The Girl Under ι

First Printing, 2022
Line Editing: Grace Michaeli

Contact: alex@authoralexamit.com
http://authoralexamit.com/

ISBN: 9798416112394

The Girl Under the Flag

Part 1

Alex Amit

Paris 1942

Top Secret 7/2/1942

From: Western Front Wehrmacht Command

To: Gestapo Headquarters, Paris

Operation Spring Breeze

Purpose: Purge of Jews from Paris.

Method: Arrest all Jews of Paris and concentrate them in the Vélodrome d'Hiver winter sports stadium, in order to cleanse the Paris area of Jews and send them to resettlement in eastern Poland.

Forces and missions: For the benefit of the operation, cooperation will be coordinated with the Paris police headquarters, which will allocate police forces to the operation. Supervision of the Paris Police is the responsibility of SS Regiment 1455.

Division 381 will serve all logistical needs during the operation.

Locomotives and train carriages for transport to eastern Poland are the responsibility of Western Front Railway Command.

Schedules:

Operation start time: 7/16/1942 at H - 04:00

SS. Telegram 344

Paris, Fourth arrondissement,

July 16, 1942, 6 am.

"According to our records, there is a missing person here. A girl, Monique, seventeen years old."

I cling as close as I can to the wall, feeling the roughness of the bricks through my thin nightgown. It seems to me that the cracks in the wall are slitting and injuring my back, but I keep myself quiet. My palms cover my mouth so I do not cry out in fear, and my eyes are wide open in panic, but it does not matter, I cannot see anything in the dark.

"I sent her early to go stand in line for flour and oil at the grocery store on Capone street," I hear my mother's voice answering the stranger through the small wooden door that hides me.

Only a few minutes, or maybe more, have passed since the loud knocks on our apartment door and the shouting: "Police, open the door!" I ran barefoot down the hall, watching Dad come out of their bedroom walking slowly, wearing his brown robe, and giving me a soothing look.

 "Quick, take Jacob," Mom shook me from my standing in the hall, holding my hand tightly and whispering for me to take him and hide.

"What about the boy, Jacob, eight years old?" There is another foreign voice, as if passing by and reading from a pre-made list, and I cling even more to the small place.

"He's in the other room with his Dad, they are packing the suitcase, tell them to speed up."

He wouldn't come with me. I rub my arm where mom held me and feel a tear running down my cheek. He'd clung to her tightly, refusing to leave her, and began crying as the knock on the door got stronger, until I had no choice but to run down the hall, leaving him hugging her leg while she tried to calm him down.

The noise of the opened door and the voices of the men at the entrance echoed in my ears as I entered the pantry, bending down and crawling into the corner of my childhood hiding place, carefully closing the wooden board behind me and resting my head on my knees in the dark. My fingers are constantly rubbing my nightgown, I mustn't make any noise.

"When will she return?"

"After she's finished, I asked her to go to my sister in the second arrondissement, so she will only be back in the afternoon."

"Do you believe her?"

Why us? Get out of here, go get another family, not us, you can go to the Jacques family, they live in the building next door, number 41, third floor, why did you choose to take us? For a moment I'm afraid I'll start screaming and I shove my palm back into my mouth, turn it into a fist and bite it until I bleed. Go to them, we have not done you any harm.

"You can ask the neighbor next

door. Go knock on her door and ask if she saw the girl coming out." The stranger continues with his horrible words.

She will protect me, she must protect me, she always allows her son to study with me, even though we are Jews and I no longer go to school. She even says that it is terrible, and that this war has been going on for too long.

I breathe quietly, another breath and another breath.

"I asked the neighbor, she says she did not see her go out this morning, and that she never sends her out so early."

Please do not search for me, please don't. My entire body cramps as I cover my ears with my palms, trying to keep the horrible sounds away as they penetrate the thin wooden board that separates me from them. For several days now, Mom has been telling Dad that there are rumors the Germans intend to send the Jews to the East, talking in whispers at the family table after dinner, making sure Jacob does not hear and start asking questions. And Dad answers in his authoritative voice that these are just rumors and that it will not happen, that we are French citizens and the Germans would not dare to do such a thing. I don't want to travel east. My fingernails grip my folded legs tightly, scratching them as I cling to the wall harder, wanting to disappear inside the wall cracks.

"Search for her."

Do not breathe, they will hear my breaths, do not move, close your eyes tightly, think about the pre-war summer, how beautiful it is in the sun. Do not scream, put your hand in your mouth again, do not shake, they will hear the tremors.

"Aren't you going to help him pack the suitcase? Only one suitcase for the family, in the East they will provide you with everything you need."

"No, I want to look after the family's silverware." I hear Mom's voice and the click of her shoes on the wooden floor in the kitchen, next to my hiding place.

"Did you find her?" The stranger raises his voice.

"She's not here and the neighbor is wrong. I sent her early in the morning. Ask the doorwoman at the entrance to the building."

"Go down and bring the doorwoman, but hurry."

Just not Odette, the doorwoman of the building. I've been scared of her since I was a kid, she's always yelling at Jacob and me. Like a tiger she lurks for us in her little room at the bottom of the stairs, where she lives, leaping towards us as we enter the big door laughing, or playing catch in the courtyard, berating us that we are not educated and making noise. To avoid shaking, I have to think of something else, not about this dark place, please don't find Odette.

"Aren't you getting dressed? Go get dressed." The voice of this terrible stranger does not stop.

"I'm waiting for them to finish packing, one more minute. Please."

A mix of footstep noises in the house, hitting the wooden floor, approaching and moving away, as though passing between the rooms. With every door slam I cringe a little more, waiting for the creak which will open the little wooden door that protects me.

"Whose shoes are these? Your daughter's? How did she go without shoes?"

The sound of something hits the floor.

"She took my shoes. Those shoes already squeeze her when she has to stand for hours."

"It's because she's a spoiled Jew."

Another sound of footsteps and another door slam and I cringe more in the dark.

"Did you see our Monique leave the building early this morning for the grocery store on Chapone Street?"

"Do not ask her, I'm asking her, have you seen the Jew girl going out? We are evacuating them."

Tears drip down my cheeks, I don't want them to look for me, I don't want to be Jewish, I want to be just an anonymous girl, why did they come at all? Why are they taking us? My body is shaking and I'm so cold.

"The rude Jewish girl? Yes, she went out this morning. I was angry with her, the little brat did not want to tell me where she was going."

Return to breathing, small breaths.

"What should we do, keep searching for her?"

Breathe quietly, do not move.

"No, we have to hurry. We have another whole truckload of Jews for evacuation. Later they will pick her up off the street and load her."

Mom's footsteps walk away from the kitchen, becoming weaker and weaker.

"Give the neighbor the key to the apartment. She'll keep it until we get back." I hear Dad say to Mom before the door slams shut. And even though I keep listening from my hiding place, I hear no more noise inside the apartment, only Jacob's cries from the staircase and Mom's soothing words until they are no longer heard either. I must not come out of my hiding place.

***

The sound of falling porcelain plates makes me jump and my head hits a hard surface, waking me up in pain. My mouth opens to scream, but I manage to control myself and the bursting cry freezes in my mouth as I hold my breath and my eyes are wide open, looking in the darkness as if trying to penetrate it through the wooden boards that close on me. Where am I?

It takes me a moment to remember where I am, and where all this darkness around me came from. My legs ache from prolonged sitting without movement and the inability to straighten them, and

I need to go to the bathroom so badly. How long have I been here? How did I let myself fall asleep after they took Mom and Dad and Jacob out of the house?

"Where did she hide her jewelry?" I recognize the voice of our neighbor Yvette, whose apartment door is across the hall. "Don't mess around, the stinky Jews will not return." She keeps talking, maybe to her son.

How can I stop the tremors? My hands hold my legs tightly while I fold into an uncomfortable sitting position with my back against the rough wall.

"And look for food too. They must have left something behind. I know she has stock for hard times." Her voice moves away along with the footsteps on the hardwood floor, and I guess she's going to look through the rooms of the house. Why are Mom and Dad not coming home to expel her? Dad would stand in the hallway with his authoritative look, and straight away she would smile and apologize, saying she did not mean to, and that she just wanted to keep things safe for us and not take anything. The creaking sounds of moving furniture on the floor penetrate through the wooden board and I remember my private diary, where is my diary?

The diary I received as a gift for my fifteenth birthday, with a brown hardcover on which I gently wrote the initials of my name in rounded letters. Every evening I wrote my hidden thoughts in it. Page after page, I told it everything that happened and sometimes drew flowers from memory. We are no longer allowed to go to the Tuileries Gardens, the sign at the entrance forbids it.

What if she discovers the diary in her search? Reads my secret words? I need it now, close to me in all this darkness and all the noises around.

My hands cover my ears, trying to get me away from this whole horrible day that won't come to an end. The porcelain plates are wildly placed on the kitchen counter above my head. Suddenly I am surprised by a flash of light that dazzles my eyes as I open my mouth without saying anything.

My eyes blink from the bright light and I want to hide, to be part of the wall, a page in my diary, a small corner in the dark, but it is too late. The light penetrates my hiding place, leaving me no place to hide anymore. My gaze rises slowly, and my eyes notice Theo, the neighbor's son. He leans on his knees next to my hiding place, holds the wooden board in his hand and looks at me with a serious look, without a smile. My eyes try to get used to the daylight as I stare at him, still sitting folded in my breached hiding place.

A few seconds of silence as we examine each other. I wait for him to do something, depending on desires and what he chooses to do, like I'm the mouse we saw some time ago. We'd played together in the courtyard of the building, and stood and laughed over it, watching it run along the wall and try to escape the grey cat. Slowly the cat approached and caught it in the corner, waiting patiently to strike the deathblow.

"Did you find her jewelry?" Yvette's voice comes from the other room and her footsteps noisily approach on the parquet, and before I can ask him not to say anything or betray me, I feel his hand resting on my lap for a moment and think he is about to pull me out. But the door slams shut and I'm in the darkness again.

"What did you find? Did you find anything?"

"No, Mom, there's nothing in the kitchen here. They left nothing except the porcelain plates."

"Didn't you find anything they hid? I'm sure she hid her jewelry, it's so typical of her."

"No, nothing, some food, that's all."

My fingers gently feel the apple he left in my lap, wrapping it slowly as if it were a precious jewel, feeling the hunger as a pain in my stomach. All I want is one bite, but I hold off as long as I can hear Yvette's footsteps in the kitchen, settling for smelling the apple and sliding it over my cheek. For some reason, its smooth touch soothes me, reminding me of the touch of the wool blanket in my bedroom, the one that covers me every night. I'll hold back and keep the apple for later.

The front door slams shut, and the noise of footsteps and the dragging of property is no longer heard. The silence has returned to the small shelter I am in, but despite my sore legs, I have no courage to go outside or even change position. How did Theo discover me in this hiding place? I must not fall asleep again.

***

What time is it? Earlier, when I pressed my ears to the wooden wall, I could hear the sounds of the street, but now I hear nothing, what does that mean? Is it night already? Maybe Mom and Dad and Jacob will be back? For a moment I think I hear footsteps in the staircase, and I press my ears tightly and listen hopefully, almost tempted to get out of this darkness I'm in. Maybe the police realized there was a mistake in the lists and sent them back home?

They would come through the door and forgive Yvette for robbing them and not guarding our apartment, as she promised, and Mom would fix the dishes in the kitchen and hug me like she used to, and she would not mind at all that we had no food left, until the next time we'd get ration coupons.

The apple? Where is the apple? It must have fallen out of my hand as I nodded off. My hands search the floor of the small space until I feel its smooth touch, and I pick it up again in my lap, promising myself to keep it for later. I'm so hungry.

Is it night already? Where are Mom and Dad? And what about Jacob? Is he still crying? If he was crowded here with me, I could sing him a lullaby and calm him down, as he liked when he was younger, before the Germans came. I used to hum to him quietly until he fell asleep.

Go to sleep my little brother

Go to sleep my little brother

Mom is making you a cake

Daddy will bring you chocolate

I want a cake so much right now;
I have not eaten one in so long.
Every Friday night we would sit
around the table, lighting candles
and singing Shabbat songs, and
Mom would give us a slice of baked
cake. The memory fills my mouth
with saliva, and I swallow it in
frustration. Since the Germans
arrived, we were almost left
without food, and on Fridays we
no longer sang, fearing that by
chance someone from the street

would hear us. Only Dad would quietly bless the food we had, and Mom, after making sure the house curtains were closed, would light two small candles she had specially hidden. By that time, we no longer had candlesticks, Mom had sold the family's silver candlesticks on the black market in exchange for a pound of meat.

For my seventeenth birthday Mom brought me a chocolate bar, I have no idea how she managed to get it or how much she paid for it. She came to me and hugged me, even though we'd had a fight the night before. She told me that I was now seventeen and mature. I hugged her back even though I was still angry with her, and so happy about the chocolate. For days I would hold back and take small bites of it, making sure to keep it as long as possible, knowing I would have no more chocolate after I finished the tablet.

One small bite of the apple, just one.

I can repeat what I learned in school, so I won't forget anything. The capital of the United States is Washington, the longest river in Europe is the Danube. The student Monique Moreno will stand in the corner and give me the note she was trying to pass to her friend. Just one more bite of the apple and I'll stop. From today on, the student Monique Moreno must wear a yellow badge attached to her clothes, and she may not play with her friends during the school break. The student Monique Moreno will not join the class tour because Jews are not allowed to enter museums. A little more of the apple. The girl Monique Moreno will walk down the street with her head down, not looking at the posters pasted on the walls, showing the Jews as rats taking over the world.

German language, I can whisper and practice my German language. Where's your ID? Where are your food stamps? Go and stand last in the line, no butter allowance remains today for the last in line. Get up against the wall as a German soldier passes by, head down you filthy Jew.

***

How long should I stay? I cannot be here anymore. The creaking of the wooden board sounds like a thunderbolt to me and I change my mind and quickly close it up again, but after few minutes my fingers open it once more.

The house is dark and quiet, and I crawl out of my hiding place, sitting on the kitchen floor. For a moment I try to stand and look out a window, but my leg muscles that had been cramped all day betray me, and I have to kneel back on the wooden floor, stretching my legs slowly and trying to listen to the sounds of the street while sitting on the floor. But my attention is on the front door. If they try to catch me now, I won't be able to escape.

The darkness of the empty apartment threatens me, but I am afraid to turn on the light. What time is it? I use my hands and lean on the windowsill to carefully peek out. The street is empty and no one is passing by. Only a streetlight illuminates the deserted sidewalk in a dim light, painting it yellowish.

The diary! I rush to my room, feeling my way in the dark and almost tripping over a pile of thrown belongings in the hall. My bed moves and my hands grope in the dark through the space next to the wall, right on the floor, relaxing only when my fingers feel its hard cover, bringing it closer to my heart as if it could provide me some protection against this whole day.

I must not turn on a light, if they know I'm here they will come again, knock on the door with their fists and shout "Police!" What should I do? Where are Mom and Dad? When will they return?

"God," I pray quietly as I lie on the floor of my room and press the diary to my chest. "I promise to be a good girl and not quarrel with them anymore when they say we should cut back. I promise, just return them to me, please, I will never shout that I am tired of being Jewish and that I am not willing to sew a yellow badge on my dress."

I have to get dressed, to be ready. The candle I found in the kitchen drawer illuminates my messy room as I search for a dress. I find my shoes lying at the entrance to the kitchen, but apart from them, the cupboards are empty. Mom's silverware is gone and so is the food from the pantry. There are only a few breadcrumbs left that I manage to scrape off the shelves with my fingers, putting them in my mouth and licking ravenously, but that does not quench my hunger. I have to keep some of the apple.

The sound of footsteps on the staircase of the building makes me jump, and I blow out the candle, standing still. Did they hear that there was someone in the house? Please, make them be Mom and Dad and Jacob. God, I promise to behave well and never quarrel with them again.

But the door remains closed and there is no key rattling in the lock, or loud knocks on the door. The steps continue to climb up the stairs as I slowly catch my breath.

I must not stay home, they will look for me, the policeman said they would pick me up. Why did Mom tell him I would go to Aunt Evelyn's? I'll go to her, she'll probably know where the police took them.

I have to hurry before they come back and pick me up. The dark stairwell looks less threatening than the empty apartment, and I go out and slam the door behind me. My hands search for the banisters as I carefully go down the dark staircase that leads to the street, my gaze focused on the dim light emanating from the open door of Odette, the doorwoman, who lives at the entrance to the building.

Paris, at night.

"Monique, stop," Odette cries, but I do not listen to her. My feet run past the open door of her room, skipping over the strip of light that is cast into the darkness of the entrance hall, and I keep on running. The fear of her spurs me on as I forcefully pull the latch of the heavy front door, open it a crack and run out into the street with only my dress on and my diary pressed against my chest. I'm too afraid she will try to catch me, and I'm not looking back.

But as soon as I slow down in the street, careful not to stumble on the pavements slippery from the light summer rain, trying to catch my breath, I notice them and I want to scream.

I have no idea what time it is, but if it's after the middle of the night, it is curfew time, and no one is allowed to be on the street, especially not a Jewish girl.

They both stand at the end of the street, wearing policeman hats and looking like dark shadows in the light of the lantern, which shines with a faint light.

Are they looking for me? Waiting to arrest me? That was what the policeman had said in the morning. My hands quickly go through my dress pockets, searching for the key to our home, realizing I forgot to take it. I have no way back. I also forgot my ID.

"A Jewish girl caught during curfew is as good as dead," Mom would scold me when I'd come home late at night, trying to close the front door as quietly as I could, knowing she was lurking for my return and that I would not be able to get away from this.

"You must not forget who you are," Dad used to tell me with a tired face as he emerged from their bedroom late at night, slowly adjusting his robe. "The situation is difficult," he added when he got in the middle of the fight between us, and Mom called on him to impose discipline on me.

"I'm not Jewish, I'm an ordinary French girl," I answered him with a stubborn face, but despite all the harsh words I said to him, refusing to look down, I was really frightened of the police. I used to get back at safe hours, sneaking through the front door of the building, passing Odette and her remarks, and sitting quietly in the staircase, waiting there for hours until it was late, and only then entering the apartment and quarrel with Mom. Dad once found me sitting in the dark on the staircase, shivering cold and waiting, and wasn't angry at me at all, he just stroked my head and said we are in a difficult time, and that Mom has enough worries besides where her daughter walks at night, and no matter what happens I must not forget who I am. I want him to stroke my head so much now, and tell me the same things, as I'm in the middle of the street in front of two cops during the curfew.

Please do not look in my direction, please do not notice me. For a moment my feet freeze in place and I almost stumble on the pavement, but manage to recover and walk a few steps towards the shadow of the building which hides me from them. Quietly I lower myself behind the entrance stairs, while my hand keeps looking in my dress pocket for my ID, but it's not there.

Where is it? Did the police take it with them in the morning? Did I forget it at home? I'm as good as dead without that beige cardboard. What would I do without my photo and my fingerprint and a blue stamp of taxes in the amount of 12 francs that Mom had paid to the clerk? I must have my ID, even though it has a large, humiliating red stamp on it: "Jew."

After the Germans arrived, we received warrants that ordered us to go to the police station. I was ashamed to go, shouting at Mom that we are proud French citizens and we have the right to refuse such humiliating instructions. What would I do now without my ID?

I have to get to Aunt Evelyn; she will find a solution. I walk against the walls of the buildings, slowly getting away from the two policemen, but there, around the corner, I hear more voices and I have no courage to keep going. All I can do is crawl between two trash cans, hide and wait for morning, exhausted, tired and hungry.

When the sun rises, I will reach Aunt Evelyn and she will help me.

***

"They're not here, the police took them," Mathilde, the doorwoman at the entrance to Aunt Evelyn's building, tells me, as she holds the heavy wooden door a crack open, preventing me from entering the building.

"Please, I'm alone, they took my parents, where did they take them?" I beg her. She's known me since I was a little girl, bouncing merrily on the street and knocking on the wooden door and shouting: "Mathilde, I've come to visit Aunt Evelyn." Too small to reach the bell.

"The police came yesterday morning and took everyone. I have no idea where, I'm sorry, I cannot help you." And she slams the big wooden door in my face.

I look to the sides, searching for a sign of French policemen or German soldiers. Maybe it's my time to be captured, I've run out of strength to keep running. At least they will take me to where Mom and Dad are, I have no place to hide.

I'd hidden among the bins until first light, shivering from every noise, and as soon as people started walking in the street I came out of hiding, careful not to run and not to arouse suspicion, constantly checking if I was being followed and looking for round helmets in the streets. But Aunt Evelyn is not here, and Mathilde doesn't let me in.

The passersby on the street ignore me, looking forward while walking, and I knock again on the brown wooden door. I have nothing to lose.

"Mathilde, please."

"Well, come in." She eventually opens the door and pulls me inside, immediately closing it with the big black latch.

"Help me, please, I have to find her, where did the police take them?"

"They were not home when the police officers came to pick them up," she surprises me as I follow her into the courtyard. She lowers her voice as she walks, looking around to make sure no one is around, not even a neighbor going down the stairs.

"I told the police they left Paris." And she walks over and moves a rickety wooden ladder that rests on a small door of a shed standing at the back corner of the yard, knocking three times on the wooden door.

"They're inside, waiting to be evacuated. Join them, and make sure to be quiet."

***

"We have no place for her."

"But Albert, she's my sister's daughter. I cannot leave her on the street."

"You heard the man from the resistance. He only has room for four people, not even one more. We have no choice, she must go."

"We have to get her in. They'll catch her."

"Do you want us all caught? Do you want us all sent to eastern Poland?"

"We will succeed in convincing him to add another person, he will agree."

"No, he will not agree, not without her having forged papers."

"I cannot leave her alone. She is my family."

"We are your family; do you want to endanger your whole family?"

"She will die here alone in the streets; she will be caught and she will die." I hear Evelyn's silent cry through the open door to a crack in the shed, but Albert does not answer her anymore, and closes the door in my face.

I stand still for a few moments, gazing at the closed door. What's the point of knocking again? They will not open up for me. Slowly I sit down on the ground, lean against the wall of the building and start crying.

It's not a loud cry, but small breaths of despair mixed with tears. If only I could be a little girl again, like I used to be. To take a walk down the streets of Paris without worries, knowing Mom is waiting for me in the warm house with the smell of cinnamon cake, lying down every night in my cozy bed. Smiling and filling up my new diary with words of imagination about what I will be when I grow up.

Sounds of footsteps are heard from the entrance of the building, but I do not raise my head, continuing to read my diary which rests on my crossed legs. I do not look, even when the sound of footsteps is already close to me, I don't care who comes to look for me and catch me. I will die soon anyway.

* * *

"Come on, hurry, what are you doing out here?" Mathilde's hand grabs my arm and she's dragging me into the interior of the building. Almost by force she puts me in her little room by the front door, quickly closes the door behind us and seats me on the wooden chair in the corner.

"What are you doing out there?"

"They are not willing to take me with them," I mumble and look down, my hands holding the diary tightly.

"Well, well." She approaches and hugs me for a moment. My hands hold her gratefully, but she

50

releases my hug and just puts her hands on my shoulders. She is not probably used to expressing feelings, or recognizing the class difference between us, which may now have been completely reversed, as I am a hunted Jew and she is safe in her little room.

"I cannot help you. I have nowhere to hide you, and if they catch me, they will kill us both," she says as she turns her back on me and walks over to the small kitchenette. She takes out a loaf of bread wrapped in brown paper, and begins to slice it, and I eagerly look at her fingers holding the bread.

"I do not know where your family is, but you cannot trust anyone, you must rely only on yourself." Her words barely reach me as she bends over and takes a jar of jam out of the cupboard, opens it, and spreads a thin layer of strawberry jam on the slices of bread.

"You must forget who you were." She repeats her words several times as she sits next to me and I hold the plate in my lap, taking small bites of the bread, savoring the sweet taste of the jam.

"Are you listening to me? You must forget who you were."

"Yes, I must forget who I am." I must change.

***

"What are you doing?"

I raise my gaze and notice him. He is about Jacob's age, but he looks more neglected as he stands and watches me curiously.

"I found this dress and I'm fixing it."

"Mother says all the Jews are dirty and it is lucky the Germans are taking them."

An hour earlier, Mathilde expelled me from her little room, forcing me to leave its safety, out into the streets and the city beyond the building's heavy wooden door. "You have to go," she told me, not before she gave me another hug and tucked an apple and two slices of jam-smeared bread, wrapped in brown paper, into my dress pocket.

"Keep the food for later, my dear child, may God be with you," she whispered as she pushed me out and made the sign of the cross in a quick motion. And I had no other choice but to start walking with my head down, among all the people returning from work on a summer afternoon.

I go down the street with no real direction, lifting my head from time to time, waiting for the policemen to pick me up. But no policeman attacks me or calls me to stop, nor do I see any German soldiers. Even when I climb several stairs at the entrance to one of the buildings and look down the street, I don't identify any blue hats of policemen blue hat or the grey-green uniform of soldiers.

The city remains the same, the people walk their same normal walk. The men in suits and hats, and the women in summer dresses. No one slows down, or breaks into a fast run, everyone gets on with their lives. Most of them don't even look at the yellow badge attached to my dress, even though it makes me feel so exposed.

It's like nothing has changed in the world since yesterday, and the police are not looking for me, and did not take Mom and Dad and Jacob to an unknown place.

I keep on moving from street to street, with no direction, until I notice them in the distance, further down Rivoli Street, and stand still. At first they look like a dark block slowly moving in my direction, approaching me step by step. But when they come close, and all the people in the street go to the sides to make room for them and the policemen guarding them, I can see their faces.

I must hide, and I bend down

behind some empty wooden food boxes that lie atop each other next to a grocery store, making sure to hide the yellow badge with my palm. Despite lowering my gaze to the pavement, trying not to stand out, I can't help it, and from time to time I sneak looks at them. They walk quietly, dead-eyed, holding their coats in their hands. Some carry heavy suitcases or a bundle packed in a piece of cloth. And only one girl walks between her two parents, giving them both her hands and bouncing cheerfully, as if she were on an afternoon walk.

As they pass me, I look down again, so as not to arouse suspicion. I hear her ask her father where they are going on this trip, and I have to stop myself from running those few steps and joining them. Just to not being alone.

It's a matter of time until they
catch me. The thought runs
through my head as they walk
down the street, and I escape into
a neglected alley beside the main
street. I have to do something; I
have to forget who I am.

Some stones in the street have
been taken out by city employees,
and I decide this is the right place
to let my diary go. I dig into the
hard ground by using a small
wooden stick and my fingers,
working quickly before anyone
notices the Jewish girl sitting in the
corner of the unfamiliar alley.

My injured fingers hold my diary
one last time, and I press it to
my chest and bring it closer to
my mouth, kissing it with my lips,

feeling the smell of the hard cover, and then placing it in the little hole I made in the ground.

 After my hands cover it with dirt and stones, I stand up and pack in the ground with my feet while looking around, trying to remember the exact location in my memory, promising myself to come back one day and get it back.

"Now it's time for the Jewish girl issue," I whisper to myself as I sit down and lean against the wall of a nearby building, trying to unravel the yellow badge from the dress with my fingernails and teeth.

"What are you doing?" the strange boy asks, surprising me, but it seems to me that my answer satisfies him. He just stays close to me, watching curiously as my fingers try to tear the sewing stitches.

"Hang on a second." He runs down the alley.

My eyes follow him, but I have to get back to my unraveling, I have to hurry before someone notices.

"Try this." He hands me a rusty nail and I thank him with a little smile.

"Are you afraid of the Jews?"

"No, why?"

"Mother says that the Jews bring diseases, like the rats, and that they want to take over the world, she saw it in an exhibition." I look up at him, trying to figure out his intentions, popping the stitches more quickly with the help of the rusty nail.

I must not think about the posters for this horrible exhibition. They have been pasted on billboards all over the city, inviting the public to come see how we have big noses and lots of money. Posters that made me hate myself and my family every time I passed them by.

"The Jews are just ordinary people," I answer him, and wonder what to do with the yellow badge resting in my palm. I despise it, but Mom had to pay for it with expensive clothing stamps instead of buying clothes last winter. I'd sat in our cold living room and watched her silently embroider them on our clothes, hating her for giving in to the Germans' rules. Where is she now?

"Mom says they're like rats, and the sign can be seen." He points with his hand, and I notice that a less-faded mark remains on the dress fabric where the yellow badge had been.

"Hang on a second," I hear him say as I try to rub the cloth and smudge the less-faded place, noticing that he is running down the alley again, dipping his hand in a bucket filled with water which lies at the entrance to one of the buildings.

"Here you go." His mud-smeared hand passes over the fabric of my dress and smears the area, painting it brown as he passes his hand over my chest, not noticing my cringe.

"Now you can't see." He steps away and carefully examines the covered

stain, while I look at my dress.
Now I'm just a normal, neglected
girl.

"Are you hungry?"

"Yes."

"Hang on a second." He turns away
from me and runs, entering the
doorway of the next building. But
after he disappears from sight and
only the sound of his footsteps
is heard, and although I am still
hungry and know I must get more
food, I get up and quickly walk out
of the alley to the main street. I
have to stay away from his mother,
even though I am not a Jew girl
anymore. I left my identity and
a buried diary under the street
stones behind me in the alley,
but the yellow badge is still in my
dress's pocket. I could not throw it
away.

Les Halles, Paris center food market,

four days later.

"She's hiding somewhere here, check between the horses." I hear the panting voices of the two policemen looking for me.

For three days now I have been hiding in the streets near the huge market building in the center of the city. Every time I hear voices coming close, I change my hiding place and try not to be noticed by anyone, silently praying while closing my eyes. For three days now I have been waiting for the dark hours, so I can go out and look for something to eat, moving carefully among the merchants who unfold woolen blankets and stay asleep on their goods stalls, guarding them from thieves like me. Every night I move slowly under the huge market construction, hiding and peeking behind the big wooden carts used to transport sacks and goods, waiting for an opportunity. A fallen vegetable, a few forgotten radishes, a slightly torn sack of potatoes that I can expand with my fingers, I will settle for anything I can lay my hand on.

After four days of running, I'm hungry and tired and dirty. Mathilde's slices of bread are a distant memory of a sweet taste, but I try not to think about them, it makes me hungrier.

For the first two days I was lucky and managed to find some cauliflower that fell from a broken wooden box and was forgotten, but that's all. Yesterday, I almost stole some carrots. I noticed a skinny merchant who'd left his cart abandoned for a few minutes. He went to greet his friends, joining them for drinks, and I tried to take the opportunity. Slowly I approached the cart while they talked, careful to stay shaded and not enter the light of the small lantern which hung over the stand.

"This Calvados is pure nectar; Pierre always has the best apples."

"For you, always the best."

"Finally, the Germans are cleaning the city."

"Yes, they show us how to lead herds in the streets, without a lot of dirt."

Under the cover of laughter, I took a few more steps towards a torn sack of carrots.

"Pour me some more Calvados."

"Now you are becoming like the Jews, wanting to rob all my property."

The sounds of laughter became stronger, allowing me to stretch my hand towards the cart, but as I pulled my hand out of the sack, holding a handful of sweet carrots, one of the sacks fell on the market floor, and Pierre's friend noticed me. Since then, they and the police have been trying to lay their hands on me.

My dress is already torn from that time I slipped on the stones as I ran at night between the aisles, escaping from the policemen's whistle and the footsteps of their hobnail boots approaching me. I managed to escape that time, but my knees have been bleeding since then, painting my legs in burgundy stripes.

Only the cargo horses do not care. They don't chase after me, allowing me to hide among them in the haystack that lies in front of them. Their soft noses sniff me curiously as they leisurely chew the straw, indifferently waiting for the end of the day. Close to each other they hide me in their presence until evening time, when they are harnessed to the merchants' carts. Then they will say goodbye to me, not before letting me stroke their noses with gentle motions, assuring me they will return tomorrow before sunrise with new merchandise.

"Shhhhh... be quiet," I whisper to them. Soon the evening will come, and I will be safe. Maybe the policemen will give up and go hunt another girl, or return to their families and to the dinner table. I must not think about food, the hunger makes it difficult for me to hide motionless. Please go away, with a little luck I will live another day.

"There she is." I hear the shout followed by a whistle from the policeman, and footsteps pounding the pavement. I rise from my hiding place and start running through the haystacks, skipping over a metal fence and not looking back, ignoring my painful knee.

I must not stop running. My feet carry me into the narrow passages between the empty boxes, panting

while passing among some sellers
who follow my run, but the steps
behind me do not give up. The
pounding of their feet hits my
ears like a speeding train moving
after me and never stopping. No
matter which aisle I choose, they
keep following me, whistling and
yelling at me to stop. I can't give
up, I run with a hunched back, so
as not to attract attention as I skip
past a pile of sacks waiting to be
thrown to the garbage, choosing
a new path and trying to listen to
the chasing voices, even though
my breathing interferes. Have they
lost me? Their voices are no longer
heard, I have to look back while I
keep on running, and then I get hit
and fall.

He's a big man, really big, sweaty,
wearing a grey tank top full of
stains and smelling of sauerkraut,

a filthy beret on his head, and his eyes looking at me with interest as I lie on the floor at his feet. He bends down to pick up the wooden crate that fell from his hands when we bumped into each other, and to my horror, I see a yellow badge on the pavement at his feet.

The big man's movement stops.

My gaze meets his as my fingers search the pocket of the dress, feeling the tear there. What can I say to him? I gasp and try to overcome the pain in my leg, ignoring the blood, but I've run out of energy to escape.

"Did you see a girl run down here?" I can hear the cops' voices on the other side of the pile of crates.

"I have not seen, ask him."

My eyes beg for mercy as I look at the big sweaty man in the grey tank top, not knowing exactly what to ask from him. Maybe he will protect me or help me, please do something. In a moment they will emerge around the corner and I will be part of a group of Jews gathered in the street, marching towards an unknown destination like a herd of cattle.

The man looks at my begging eyes and through the narrow aisle over my shoulder, seeking those who are chasing me. After a second, without saying a word, his huge arms, which until then had loaded empty wooden boxes into a grey pickup, grab me as if I'm a sack of potatoes. With one push he throws me into the van's trunk and I hit the hard metal floor, fighting not to scream from the intensity of the pain.

"Have you seen a girl running here?" I hear them panting while they speak to him, as I crouch in the trunk, hiding behind the wooden crates that he continues to load.

"Gypsy girl?"

"We suspect she's Jewish, we are catching them all."

"She was really stinking; she passed me and ran that way."

They do not even answer him, only the sounds of their shoes are heard moving away from me, mingling with the thumping of wooden crates which are loaded on the van at a steady pace, building me a growing protective wall, while I lie on the cold metal floor, letting my breath relax a little.

Finally, I hear the trunk door slam shut and the twilight which has penetrated through the opening is replaced by darkness, and after a few minutes the pickup engine makes a rumbling noise and we start driving. The bumps of the shaky vehicle on the pavement stones hurt me, and I try to sit so as not to get hit by the metal floor.

I have no idea where he's taking me, but I can't think about it right now.

Why has the car stopped? My ear presses against the metal side of the trunk, trying to listen to the sounds outside. The van door opens and closes, shaking the van slightly. I can hear footsteps nearby, talking and laughing, is he

alone? Is there anyone else with
him? Did anyone wait for him?
What are they planning for me?

The creaking of the trunk door
and the noise of the crates being
moved makes me jump and I
notice his silhouette in the dark.

"You can come out." But I'm afraid
to, I feel safe here.

"You can come out now, it's safe,"
he repeats himself and gives me
his hand.

My palm disappears in his big hand
as he helps me stand on the street,
supporting me for a moment as
I try to straighten my sore legs.
Even though we are already out of
the market, the smell of his body
remains as strong and unpleasant
as before. We are still in Paris,
but in another neighborhood I do

not know. The street is narrow and almost completely dark in the evening, and I cannot read its name from the small sign painted at the end of the nearest building. Where am I?

I try to look around, but he rushes me. A barrel thrown in the street, a wooden cart tied to a stand, several posters taped to the wall expressing appreciation for the government's achievements, and one streetlamp scattering a dim light. That's all I get to see. Where did the man he was talking to go? The one I'd heard while in the car?

"Follow me." The big man enters the nearest building.

My foot stumbles when I bump into the first step in the dark and I hit the wall, trying to stabilize myself with my hands, but he does not stop and I have to follow him into the dark stairwell. The creak of his shoes on the wooden boards is clearly heard, where is he taking me? My hand holds the simple railing firmly, leaning on it for support as I get ready to turn around and run away.

His place is small, much smaller than our apartment. Does he live here? Only one room without an entrance hall, and that's it. First he goes to the window and closes the curtain tightly, and only then does he turn on the light. I can still hear his breaths from the climb, as I watch him arrange the blankets on the metal bed, turning his back to me. In one corner there is a bathroom niche, a clothesline tied with several clothespins, a kitchen corner, two wooden shelves, a small table and three chairs, a tall, narrow wooden closet, and the iron bed next to the wall by the window. The big man turns around and faces me.

We inspect one another for the first time after those few seconds in the market. He is still big and sweating from the summer heat, in the same dirty tank top with the smell of sauerkraut, and the beret that had previously been on his head lies on the small table, but still he's not smiling at me.

"Sit." He hands me a chair, places it in the center of the room in a clumsy motion, and I sit down, watching the cream paint peeling off the walls. What shall I tell him if he starts asking me questions? But he stays silent, still checking me, shifting his gaze from my messed-up hair, down my filthy, torn dress, to my bare feet with clotted streaks of blood, and I look down.

"Your dress, take off your dress." I hear the words coming out of his mouth, and slowly grow terrified.

Can I escape? Can I get up from the chair and run to the door? Did he lock the door? Where's the key? Why didn't I notice? Why did I follow him up the stairwell and not escape into the street? Why is this happening to me? Where is Mom? What should I do?

I give him a questioning look.

"Take off your dress," he repeats and reaches out his hand. I freeze, so cold.

In a slow motion I get up from the chair, go to the corner of the room, turn my back to him and open the buttons one by one. A tear goes down my cheek, I cannot do it, why is he so big? I don't deserve this.

The dress is sliding from my hands to the floor and I imagine I hear the noise of the fabric hitting the wood like a gunshot. Sometimes, in the evening, I would hear shots from the window. I sit down on the floor and cringe. My stomach becomes a lump of pain.

In slow motion I turn to him in my bra and panties, covering as much of my body as I can, and give him a pleading look. I have no strength to fight him, nor to escape.

"The dress, bring me the dress." I kneel on the floor and carefully gather the cloth with my fingers, rolling it into a lump and placing it in the palm of his hand, protecting my body as much as I can with my other hand and looking at him. Why is he doing this to me?

***

When will he return? Will he return alone? I must be ready.

I have no idea how long it's been since he took the dirty dress from my trembling hands and left. He bundled it in his huge palm, smiled at me and walked out the door, leaving me kneeling on the dirty wooden floor with only a bra and panties covering my body. Before I could escape, I heard the sound of the lock imprisoning me.

What should I do? How should I prepare myself? I must get out of here. Carefully I move the curtain that covers the window and watch the dark street. The streetlight is too dim and I'm not sure if there are two people standing in the dark entrance of the next building or if it's just my imagination, but I step back, afraid they'll see me peeking out of the window.

The door, is there another key in the room? How can I get out onto the street like this? In just a bra and panties? I have to find something to wear, but the door is locked and my fingers searching the high shelf next to the door can't find a key. There are footsteps in the stairwell, run away! And I quickly get away from the door, sitting on the iron bed, not on the bed, I have to stand, or sit on the chair, the main thing is to be ready.

It's not him, it's someone else,

the steps continue on. I must do something, there is a brown bag with bread on the kitchen counter, but despite my hunger, I don't have the courage to eat, I'm too nervous, I want to scream.

Will he do to me what my mother always scared me about? I'll die, it's better for me to die, or defend myself and die, a knife, in the kitchen drawer there is a knife, I'll use it. Again I hear steps up the stairs, be prepared, like this, when I sit at the end of the bed, my back close to the wall, holding the knife tightly in my hand, hidden behind my back, I must stop shaking, there is a key turning in the lock.

***

"It's the best I've been able to get." He places a package wrapped in newspaper, tied with a simple rope, on the chair. But I do not move from my seat at the end edge of the bed, I must be ready. My palm holds the knife tightly behind my back until my muscles tremble from the tension.

"What is it?"

"I got you another dress, more or less the same size."

I slowly get off the bed. The noise of the metal springs rings in my ears as I carefully approach the package. My hand is still holding the knife behind my back, ready for any surprise, but he's not trying to catch me. With a shaking hand I place the knife on the floor and open the bag, keeping the knife close to me. In the package there is a simple grey women's dress, and I press it to my body in order to hide my nakedness.

"I hope it's good enough."

"Thanks."

"You need to clean up," he says, and turns to the small bathing corner, collecting ready-made soap and placing it in my hand. If he notices the knife lying on the floor, he ignores it and says nothing. He simply turns his back to me and goes to the kitchenette, starting to arrange groceries. I'm so hungry.

How can I clean up next to him? I can't go to the bathroom corner to wash myself, knowing his eyes will look at my body. I can't do it, it's too much for me.

As he turns from the kitchen corner, probably wondering about

the sound of breathing he heard,
he finds me sitting on the wooden
floor and crying. Without a word
he walks to me, picks me up like
I'm a rag doll and takes me to the
bathroom. After placing me next to
the bucket of water, he makes sure
I am stable enough and puts the
soap in my hand again, but I keep
standing still with a begging look,
smelling the strong scent of his
body.

"We'll figure something out," he
replies though I've said nothing,
and after a few seconds of
thinking, he loosens the clothesline
that hangs on the wall, pulling it to
the other side. Then he brings in
a sheet from the small closet, and
hangs it, giving me some privacy.

With my back to him and with
closed eyes, as if I was a little girl

hiding my eyes with my palms and not wanting to be seen, I start cleaning myself. The rough soap scratches my skin and hurts me, when will all this end? What will he do to me? I must not think about it now, I must hurry to clean up and get dressed, to be safe again.

My hands are still shaking from the cold bathwater, as my fingers struggle with the buttons of the grey dress. I hate this color. Since it all started two years ago, this color makes me shiver. Endless rows of German soldiers wearing grey-green uniforms, marching on the Champs Elysees, ignoring the shocked people watching them in fear. They looked like giants to me with their helmets and rifles, like this man. I'm afraid of him too, despite the smell of cooked food slipping through the sheet that hides me. Will he give me some of his food?

Two plates are waiting on the table, and we sit and eat the stew he has prepared in silence. I think he even put some meat inside, I have not eaten meat in so long. After I finish all my food, carefully cleaning it all with the spoon, as much as I can, he pours another heaping spoonful of stew into my plate and I finish it all too. Doesn't he want to ask me some questions? Where is my family? Why am I running away? What is it like to be a stinking Jew?

"Thanks." I stand in the corner of the room next to the wall as he arranges the bed, taking another thin blanket out of the closet and places it on the floor, straightening it gently with his big hands.

"You are welcome."

"They took my parents and I ran away."

"I know."

"I was a normal girl, and I have a little brother, Jacob, they also took him. The police just came to our house a few days ago, and I've been running ever since." I can't stop talking, even though he does not ask. In peaceful movements he arranges the bed and the blanket on the floor and goes to the bathroom corner, closing the sheet curtain behind his back as he cleans himself, and I look at the iron bed and the neat blanket on the wooden floor. Will he attack me? Can I trust him?

"I went to school and I speak German and some English, and

I was the best in my class, but one day they said I couldn't go to school anymore, and I was sitting at home, thinking that I hated my mother, pretending I was already asleep when she would come into my room at night to talk to me, and now I miss her so much."

I keep on talking, not knowing if he is already asleep or lying in the dark, looking at the ceiling and listening to me. Maybe my words are keeping him up?

The feeling is strange to me and I can't sleep. My eyes are wide open in the dark as I lie in a foreign bed next to an unfamiliar man who lies on the floor next to me. Every now and then I move my body until I hear the creaking of the metal springs of the bed, can I trust him and close my eyes? I want to ask for his name, and why he saved me, and what happened to the yellow badge that was lying on the floor, and how the cops did not notice it, but I am embarrassed and instead keep on talking about myself in the dark. Maybe he is listening.

***

Latin Quarter.

My eyes slowly open to the morning sun, searching for the floral curtains of my room. In a moment, Mom will enter my room and get mad at me because it's late and I have to get up and go to the grocery store on Capone Street, to stand in the endless line for flour, or oil. In a moment I'll start arguing with her that because we are Jews I have to stand at the end of the line until nothing is left. These are not the curtains of my room.

The blanket is tossed aside, and my bare feet touch the floor, feeling the rough wood while my eyes search around, looking for escape routes.

The small room is quiet and has no one but me. The table in the kitchen is still in the same place and the three chairs have not been moved either. The sheet placed on the clothesline for privacy is rolled aside and there is no one behind it, but the blanket that was spread out last night at the foot of the bed is folded on the side of the room beside the wall.

It takes me a while to calm down. Where did he go? Why did I not wake up when he got up? I anxiously check the room, slowly walking around and looking for suspicious signs.

"I'll be back in the evening." That's all he left me in a sloppy note written on a piece of cardboard on the kitchen table, next to a plate with two slices of bread and a pear. Yesterday's knife was back in the drawer, but I pull it out again, placing it on the table within reach of my hand.

Is everything all right?

The daylight penetrates the small window through the closed curtain, illuminating the apartment in a yellowish hue, and it looks slightly larger and more neglected. The peeling stains of the paint from the walls are noticeable, and the brown door also needs painting. The kitchen has dark marks, and the wooden floor is not as smooth as in our house, but I do not care about any of that. I have food here and I'm less scared than I've been in the last few days, that's enough.

One slice of bread for now, and the other slice of bread I'll eat at noon. I put the pear in my dress pocket, in case of emergency, and I allow myself to cut another thin slice of bread, convincing myself that he won't notice when he returns in the evening. What time is it?

When I pull back the curtain, I can see the street in daylight. A man is walking by and a boy plays in the street with a ball, throws it on the wall and manages to catch it. I could not keep Jacob.

Why didn't I insist as Mom told me to? Why didn't I pull him with me, ignoring his cries? We could be here together. With food and a place to sleep. I could look after him, show Mom that I'm helping. She always asked me to take care of him and I started arguing with her, and now they are gone.

My face is buried in a blanket while I cry and my body shakes and can't calm down, as much as I try to convince myself that they are OK. It's my fault Jacob is not here with me, in this small room, with food. If they return, I promise to myself that I will take care of him, wherever we go.

***

"We have to go," he tells me in the evening, after I waited for hours in the dark apartment. I leaned against the window for most of the day, pulling the curtain slightly aside and watching the street for signs of danger, searching for policemen in blue uniforms or German soldiers wearing round helmets. Every now and then I left my position by the window and went to the locked door, bringing my ear to the keyhole and trying to hear if there were any steps coming up the stairs, stopping by the door, but the stairs were quiet.

Finally I notice the lights of the pickup truck emerging into the alley, and the vehicle disappears from my sight as it is probably parking near the entrance, I take the knife and wait close to the door, ready for anything.

The big man walks in and prepares dinner for both of us. He keeps quiet while eating and says nothing, even if he notices that I took a slice from his bread. Once more he serves me an extra helping of the stew after I clean the plate with my spoon, but at the end of the meal, after placing the dishes in the sink, he turns around and stands in front of me.

"We have to go."

"Where?"

"To people I know, they will take care of you."

I must trust him, he is a good man, he will take care of me.

Like an obedient Jew I do not say a word. I get up and walk to the front door, giving one last look at the room that had been my shelter for a day. The knife lies on the counter, I wish I could hide it in my dress pocket, but it is too late now. At least I have a pear and a slice of bread.

He takes a look into the staircase, checks that no one is there, and before we go out of the building into the street, he places his hand on my arm and stops me at the dark entrance, checking that the street is empty of people. Inside the back of the van, behind the pile of boxes, he spreads an old blanket on the floor of the trunk, and I sit on it, but then he surprises me.

"Do not take it off during the ride." He pulls a dark blindfold from his

pocket and ties it around my eyes
before I crawl into my hiding place.

"Why?"

"That's the way it must be."

"Will they do something to me?"
My fingernails scratch my palm.

"You are safe, everything is OK."

And the trunk door slams and
locks, leaving me in double
darkness. My fingers carefully feel
the blindfold cover my eyes as I
breathe heavily. Where am I being
taken? What will he do with me?

He's not a bad man, he'll protect
me. The jumps of the van and
the noise of the engine do not let
me relax, not even when I try to
quietly sing a lullaby, and not even
when the van stops and I hear

voices in German. My body tenses and my mouth opens to scream, everything is not OK.

***

"Where to?" the German man asks him in bad French.

"I bring supply to the market."

"Why are you going at such a late hour?"

"I have to get a shipment of chickens."

"Do you have certificates?"

My ear is close to the metal side of the trunk, but I do not listen to him and the German stranger's conversation, but to the other voices around the vehicle, walking and speaking to each other in German.

"Do you think we'll go out this weekend?"

"Light up under the trunk. I don't think they'll let us out."

"I'm tired of checking all those cars."

"What is he carrying in the trunk?"

"Did you see how big he is? How did he get into this small van?"

"Maybe he's smuggling something?"

"This big one? He can smuggle all the Jews of France under his shirt."

"And there will be room left for

some resistance fighters."

"I hate the resistance; they scared the hell out of me."

"Shall we check the trunk?"

For two years now I have been shaking in fear of the German soldiers. Every time I go out into the street, I look for the grey-green uniforms, afraid to meet them on my way. My eyes scan for round helmets, and if I notice one, I look for another way to go. For two years now, I've had nightmares, dreaming of them stopping me in the street and putting me against the wall. I don't dare walk by the Opera and Concord Square, where the German Headquarters is located. I try to listen to every word while my hands tremble.

Everything will be alright, the big man will save me, the people he's taking me to will save me, someone will save me. What are they saying?

"Let our stupid sergeant decide."

"Yes, he thinks he can speak French."

"Or detect French smugglers."

"I hope he lets us go out this weekend."

"You can go." I hear the sergeant in his bad French. Please don't change your mind.

"Have you ever dated a French girl?"

But my ears don't hear the rest of their conversation, while the van continues along the way until it stops again. This time, the big man gives me a hand to help me get out of the trunk, supporting me as I get down with shaky legs, searching for stable ground and walking slowly with my eyes covered. Only weak machine noises can be heard around me, where is he taking me?

"Be careful, there are stairs going down." My small hand is holding his big hand, can I trust him? Will I hear German words again?

***

Philip

"Sorry, we have no place for her."

My fingers grip the black blindfold
I've just removed from my eyes,
while trying to adjust to the light of
the yellow ceiling lamp, examining
the interior of the basement and
the stranger who does not bother
to look at me.

He's wearing brown pants and a
white tank top; his dark hair is in
a quiff and he's a little older and
a little taller than me. He stands
in front of us for a moment, looks
at me for a split-second, and then
turns his back and continues his
business inside the dirty, machine-
laden workshop. My eyes look at
his back and the pistol in his belt.

"Please, you must help me." Even though he is not looking, my eyes beg him as I raise my voice, trying to overcome the noise of the rattling machines around.

He looks up to me, while holding a printed poster in his dirty hands, as if noticing my presence for the first time.

"I'm sorry, since the Gestapo started the big deportation operation, we have a lot of fugitives. The whole resistance is full of Jews trying to get out of Paris, to the south or to cross the border into neutral Spain. You are not the only one."

"They took my family."

"I'm sorry, really, but I have no hiding places left, and the roads are full of German army checkpoints. The escape routes to the south are closed." He turns his back to me again.

"I have nowhere to go." I raise my voice and talk to his back while he is busy with the printing machine, hitting hard on one of the handles.

"Maybe in a few months, things will change, but until then, I can't help you, I'm sorry." He tries to shake the handle by force.

"They will kill me." I approach him and place my hand on his back. He must hear me, but he does not answer. His brown eyes look at me sadly for a moment, but then he turns to the printing machine again, striking the metal handle once more and cursing it.

"I'm willing to do anything you ask." I have nothing left to lose, this basement with this man who carries a gun in his belt, and the noise of the machines in the background, are my last chance to live.

"I'm sorry, really, I can't get you out of Paris." And he turns his back to me for the last time, moving away from me, and I look at the back of his neck and at the printing machine that emits paper leaflets at a monotonous pace, another leaflet and another and another.

"I can give you some food I have," he turns to me.

"No thanks, I'll manage."

No one will help me, not this man nor anyone else. What will another meal do for me? The black blindfold in my hand suddenly seems like a pleasant place to sink into, to wrap myself in the darkness.

I turn to the big man who has been standing on the sidelines all this time, handing him the piece of black cloth, but he ignores my hand and walks to the young man. He puts his huge arm around his shoulder, and they whisper with their backs to me, turning and looking at me occasionally.

"Do you speak German?" The young man approaches me, asking in bad German.

"Yes, I speak German."

"How good?"

"As a native language."

"How do you know German so well?"

"My family had a business in

Germany when I was a child, so we lived there for a few years, until 1933, when the situation became problematic and my father sold his factory, got us out of there and back to France." I answer him in German, not sure he understands me, while he stands close to me and his eyes check me out.

"Do you want me to sing you a song in German?"

"Do you read and write in German?"

"As I told you, it's a native language for me."

He gives me the poster, pulls a pencil out of his pocket and hands it to me.

"Write."

"What do you want me to write?"

"Whatever you want."

Stand up, damned of the Earth

Stand up, prisoners of starvation

Reason thunders in its volcano

This is the eruption of the end.

Of the past let us make a clean slate

Enslaved masses, stand up, stand up.

The world is about to change its foundation

We are nothing, let us be all.

My fingers write the words of

the International, the socialist movement in France, on the back of the poster. Translated into German, in as round and beautiful handwriting as I can. My hand holds the paper on a metal plate of the printing machine, which keeps working and shaking as I'm writing, and I mumble the words as they are written.

"Here." I give him the piece of paper.

He glances at the written words for a second and stuffs it in his pocket, looking at me again.

"And are you Jewish?"

"Yes."

"You can call me Philip."

"My name is Monique." Maybe

I've got a chance, is Philip his real name?

"Please sit here." He grabs my arm, not by force or violence, and leads me to a simple metal chair which stands against the wall, taking a pile of papers from it and ordering me to sit.

"Wait here."

My eyes follow him as he approaches another man in the corner of the basement, whom I had not noticed until now. Tall and thin, hunched over a wooden table laden with papers, stamps, cutting tools and ink jars. The tall man sits with his back to me, concentrating on his work by the table, until Philip leans over his shoulder and talks to him. They both look at me. He thinks for a moment, takes something out of the desk drawer, gets up and leaves his cluttered desk, standing in front of me.

"Are you Jewish?"

"Yes."

"What is your name?"

"Monique."

"What's the last name?"

"Moreno."

"What are you praying for on Friday?"

"Blessed are You, Lord our God, King of the universe, who has sanctified us with His commandments, and commanded us to kindle the light of the holy Shabbat." And I remember Mom standing by the candles and blessing in her quiet voice while Dad stood next to her with a look of pride on his face.

"You bless before or after lighting the candles?" The stranger interrupts my thoughts.

"After."

"And what do you do with your hands?"

"I cover my face with them." I've got tears in my eyes thinking of Mom.

"Why are you crying? Are you stressed?"

"No."

"So why are you crying?"

"Just a memory." I must not show weakness, they will expel me.

"What do you prepare for Passover soup?"

"Kneidlach."

"How do you make them?"

And I explain how Mom would get matzah flour and eggs and oil, when it was still possible, and add a little salt, and how the whole kitchen would be filled with their smell when they were cooked in hot water. I used to taste some of them from the strainer basket, and Mom would pretend she was angry at me, but not really. Where had the police taken them?

He then lets me read prayers from a small prayer book he holds in his hand, examines whether I can read the Hebrew prayers, and I read every page he opens to him, until finally he turns his back to me and walks over to Philip, who stands aside, leaning on one of the machines, watching me all this time as I've been tested.

"I believe her, but she's too young."

"I'm nineteen years old." I turn my gaze to Philip, looking straight at him.

"She doesn't look nineteen to me."

"I just look younger."

"She will not succeed, it's too dangerous."

"I will succeed."

The tall man looks at me with anger for my interrupting his words, but Philip continues to look at me with interest.

My eyes are fixed on the wheels

of the machine that keep turning, while Philip and the tall man turn their backs to me again and argue. What else can I say that will change their minds? I have run out of other options, I depend on their mercy.

"Maybe we can help you."

I want to hug him, or fall at his feet and kiss them, but I'm afraid that tomorrow he will change his mind and I'll find myself alone again, and I just look down and say nothing.

"In the coming days we will contact you and see how we can help you." He ends the conversation between us and returns to the printing machine.

"Come with me." The big man with the dirty shirt is waiting for me, but for a moment I stand still, looking at Philip's back and the gun in his belt, wondering if I can trust him, even a little bit.

On the way back to town, blindfolded in the trunk of the bouncing van, along with crates of chickens, I sing to myself the Shabbat songs we used to sing as we sat together around the table, letting the tears come and soak in the black blindfold, and when we lie down to sleep in the apartment, I whisper "Good night" to the big man, feeling a little more secure and a little more protected.

***

"Filthy Jew."

The scream that is heard in the room is mine, as I am thrown from the bed to the floor, and a hand grabs my hair tightly and drags me to the wall, forcibly pinning me to the peeling yellow cracks. I scream again, trying to wake up and figure out where I am.

"Where is he?" the man throwing me against the wall shouts in German, his hand resting on my neck and strangling me. I can barely breathe.

"Who are you looking for?" I answer him in tears.

"Where is the man who lives here?" And his hand tightens around my neck and I gargle words and try to breathe. My eyes search the room for the big man who will protect me, but to my horror, I notice a soldier in a green grey uniform and a round helmet standing by the closed door, holding a gun in his hand.

The hand that close on my throat releases me a bit and his evil face come close to me, stinking of tobacco.

"Where is he?" he yells at me.

"I do not know where he is," I bitterly weep. Where is the big man? What happened when I slept? Why is he not here to help me?

"You liar," he slaps me in the face, and I scream. "We saw you together, you are a member of the resistance with him, where is he?" He slaps me again.

"I'm not in the resistance." I cry, feeling the pain of the slap. Who betrayed me? Did Philip with the gun in his belt betray me? Why did he do this to me? I can't take it anymore.

"You're lying, you are a filthy lying Jew, they saw you praying, where is he?"

"I do not know where he is." My words barely come out against his tight hand and the tears blur my vision, where is the man? I don't want to die.

"Last chance, where is he?" His awful hand grips my hair tightly and I scream again as he lowers me to the floor, my head almost hits the wooden floor.

"Please, I don't know." I look at his brown shoes and the hem of his coat, see my tears wetting the parquet in small circles and hold my breath for a kick to come.

"You don't know where he is?"

"I'm just a French girl, please."

"Last chance, where is he?"

"I do not know, please."

"Kill her." His whisper is heard to the soldier who is standing in the doorway and I breathe quickly, hear his footsteps approaching and see the tips of his black army boots. My eyes close as I feel the cold barrel touch my head and wait for the black to arrive. Maybe it's better that way, to stop this awful place I'm in, it hurts so much.

***

Silence,

And the silence goes on,

And the hand that grabbed my hair and nape slowly lets go and releases me,

And the gun barrel is no longer touching my head.

And I hear footsteps and a door opens, and slowly I open my eyes, still seeing the old parquet floor of the apartment, which the morning sun paints in a light shade of brown. The little circles of my tears are still visible, but the black soldier's shoes are gone and the brown shoes of the man who hit me are gone too. I do not dare to look up, knowing that they are still in the room and having fun, playing with the Jewish girl before the final execution.

"It's OK, drink now." A huge hand rests on the back of my head and even though I flinch in fear, he does not hurt me. And a simple glass of wine is served to my lips and I take small sips, doing what I am told, trying to get used to the bitter taste which is combined with the sour smell of cabbage.

"It's OK, it's over, you were OK." And I look up and see the soldier next to the horrible man in the coat, standing at the door and looking at me, but they no longer look at me in hatred. The big man's hand supports me, keeping me from collapsing on the floor, as he hugs me and hold the glass of wine to my mouth. "Drink, let the breath come back."

Later on he walks over and confides in them, as they look at me placing the glass of wine on the floor, looking down and staring at the rays of the sun that penetrate the wine and create small waves of cheerful burgundy on the floor, as if it does not care what happened here minutes before. And when I raise my head and look at the door, the terrible people have gone, and the door is closed. I haven't even heard the sound of it slamming shut.

***

The big man gets me up from the floor and supports me, lifts the kitchen chair that was turned upside down when they dragged me by my hair from the bed and slammed my body against the wall. He arranges it in place and sits me down.

After he makes sure I'm fine and I'm not going to fall on the floor again, he gently touches my shoulders for encouragement and turns his back on me. His hands take the loaf of bread out of the paper bag in the kitchen and start slicing it.

Two slices of bread on a plate, smeared with butter and a bit of strawberry-flavored jam, bitter in my mouth with the taste of my tears, a slice of yellow cheese, a glass of sweetened milk, and two cubes of chocolate substitute.

"Why did you let them?" The pain is clear in my voice, I feel unsafe in this place.

"We had to."

"Who is 'we'?"

"They will explain it to you in the evening."

"What will happen to me in the evening?" Will they play at killing me again? The lump of cheese sticks in my throat.

"In the evening we go again."

"To the same place?" The place where they don't want me? To the man who told me he was sorry? To the same road? With the checkpoint of the German soldiers, who didn't open the trunk of the van just because you are so big? What if this time there will be other soldiers? Will I die in the evening instead of dying in the morning? And if I tell you what I heard; will you cancel the ride? And then I'll walk the streets until they catch me? It's hard for me to swallow the sweet slice of bread.

"You'll know in the evening where you are going, it does not matter." Maybe it really does not matter, it's just a matter of time before someone catches me and kills me.

"Do not open for anyone and wait for me in the evening," he tells me after the meal ends in silence, and he clears the dishes and gets ready to go. I do not want to be left alone.

After I hear the door slam, I go to clean up and scrub myself. Will anyone come in and surprise me?

The knife is within reach of my hand as I clean myself, even as I peek into the street through the open curtain, jealous of the young girl walking without fear, even when I hear footsteps in the stairwell. I come close to the door and try to listen. All day the knife is in my hand and I'm ready for anything, with the pear and the two slices of bread in my dress pocket. I'm ready all the time.

***

"We have to go."

Since this morning I have been afraid of these words, knowing they will come at the end of the day. My thoughts are constantly on the German soldiers that will stop us on the way, and the questions I will hear through the thin wall of the trunk. Will they believe him?

"Go inside and sit." The trunk door closes behind me, imprisoning me again, blindfolded. My hands stabilize myself for sitting. It's too late for second thoughts.

The pungent smell of gasoline of the engine carries in the air, as the van goes down the stone road, shaking me inside the cramped trunk. I must think of something nice, like pre-war summer and vanilla ice cream. I must not think about ice cream, I just need to relax and breathe quietly, stop listening to all the noise outside, breathe and count for myself. Why did the van stop?

His big hand leads me slowly down the stairs, and the smell of print rises in my nose, even though I cannot hear the sounds of yesterday's machines.

"You're back."

His fingers gently remove the blindfold, placing it in my hand. The gun is still stuck in his belt and he is close to me, looking into my eyes which are again trying to adapt to the burst of light of the yellow ceiling lamp.

"Yes, I'm back."

"Are you fine?"

"Yes, I'm fine." Your people have done terrible things to me.

"Do you want to know why we did it?"

"No, it's OK." Because you, like them, want to see if you can trust the Jewish girl or accuse her in treason. We are always suspicious of something.

"How old are you?"

"Nineteen years old."

"You are not nineteen, how old are you?"

"Seventeen years old."

"Why did you lie to me?"

"Because I want to reach the age of nineteen."

Philip silently looks at me, as if thinking what to do with the Jewish girl standing in front of him, and I stare back.

"We had to make sure you were not a Gestapo agent, one who would betray us all."

"I had a father and mother and Jacob that the Germans took. Do you still think I'm a Gestapo agent?"

"You'll have to learn to be more polite, and don't lie to me anymore." He turns and walks to the table at the end of the room. "Come here."

I sit down in front of him on the wooden chair. My hands are under my thighs, feeling the roughness of the wood, but close to the knife hidden in the dress pocket, along with the pear and the two slices of bread.

"You have two options," Philip leans towards me and looks into my eyes, putting his hands on the table as if he wants to show me that his intentions are good. I stare at the color print stains on his fingers.

"First option, we can take you back to Paris, you will go your own way, you'll probably try to get to the south on your own and maybe you'll succeed in crossing the border into Spain. With all my heart I'd wish you good luck. I will also give you some food."

"And the other option?"

"You will join us."

"Which means?"

"Everything we need."

"And who are you?"

"We are the fighters for free France."

"Will I die?"

"Maybe, maybe I will die too, life is given to those who are willing to fight for it."

"I want to live."

"I cannot guarantee you that."

I can feel the metal touch of the knife in my pocket. I am tired of running by myself, living from minute to minute in such fear.

"What would I do for you?"

"You will bring us information about the Germans."

"I'm scared of them; they will kill me."

"They'll probably kill us all."

"I'm Jewish."

"You'll have to forget who you are, you'll become someone else."

"I hate who I am."

"Good."

Philip smiles a little at me, for the first time since noticing me last night, and turns around and calls out to the tall man, who is leaning over his stamping table, busy with his work and ignoring us. The stamp man delays for a moment while concentrating on some document, then he takes a cardboard box off the shelf above him and takes out a camera.

"Come over here, stand by the white wall. I need to photograph you for a fake ID."

As I get up from the chair and try to digest what I have chosen, I turn to look at the front door of the basement, searching for the big man who brought me here, wanting to thank him for saving my life. But he is not here anymore.

***

A New Life

May, 1943

Secret

5/3/1943

From: Western Front Wehrmacht Command

To: 34 Corps Paris

Reorganization, Regulation 53

Purpose: Paris Area is Declared a recovery home base for German army troops.

General: The remaining divisions of Rommel's African Corps are retreating from North Africa, under pressure from American and British forces.

The number of casualties in battles against the Russian army on the Eastern Front is steadily rising.

Therefore, Paris will be declared a recovery home base for German army troops.

Method: Regulation 53 will replace Regulation 15.

German soldiers throughout the Paris area will be allowed to purchase goods at local stores. Local Army Headquarters will select and approve stores according to their needs.

Food rations: Issuance of food ration certificates for the selected stores is the responsibility of Logistics Division 221.

SS. Telegram 821

Paris, May 1943

"ID, please."

My fingers pull the ID out of my leather bag, and I hand it to him, watching as he examines it carefully. He is taking his time, checking all the details and stamps, reviewing the picture and comparing it to my face while looking at me.

"Name?"

"Monique." Philip insisted I not change my name, so I would not be confused when I got nervous.

"Last name?"

"Otin."

"Date of birth?"

"December 14, 1925."

"How do you know German so well?"

"I grew up in Strasbourg."

"That's German territory today, why are you in Paris and not with us in Germany?"

"Dad had a lumber business, and Mom was a teacher, and I grew up there, but in 1937 Dad wanted to grow the business, and we moved to Dunkirk."

"Why Dunkirk?"

"It will not work. They will never believe me." My eyes look at Philip, sitting on the other side of the wooden table, examining me with a serious look.

"Don't stop; keep answering me."

"They will check and find that I'm lying, and kill me."

"They cannot check; thanks to the American bombers, they have nowhere to check. Strasbourg City Hall was bombed during an American raid a year ago. They tried to hit the railways and missed, destroying City Hall. What did you do in Dunkirk?"

"We were in Dunkirk until May 1940 when the Germans invaded."

"You can't recite your story; you must fill it with emotion. There will be a German investigator sitting in front of you, not me, you must speak emotionally. You must imagine that I am that German soldier who hates you."

"We lived in Dunkirk until three years ago, May 1940, when you invaded France and Belgium." Most of the time, I think he hates me.

"And what happened then?"

"They will not believe Dunkirk, why not somewhere else?"

"Because the German guns destroyed Dunkirk, not a single piece of paper was left there. Go on talking, how did you get to Paris? Do you want the German to believe you? Where are your emotions?"

"When the German army broke through the lines of defense, Dad decided we had to escape, they woke me early in the morning. When I got out of the house, the car was already fully loaded, everything Mom and Dad could pack in a hurry. We tried to escape to the south, but on the way, they were killed."

"What happened?"

"A plane. On May 23, one of your airplanes killed them."

"Watch your tone here; you are speaking about the German army."

"Sorry, I apologize."

"How did it happen?"

"A German Stuka passed by and fired at the convoy of refugees we were in, just like that." And I close my eyes and imagine the story, getting the words out slowly and emotionally.

"We'd been on the roads for two days by then, strolling down a narrow road full of cars and people and horses with carriages. The cars' roofs were loaded with mattresses and suitcases tied with ropes. The horses walked so slowly, and the air was constantly filled with the smell of fear."

"Keep on talking."

"An endless convoy headed south; I can remember the sun; it was so hot that day. Every now and then, we had to move to the side of the road, to allow a group of dirty soldiers sitting in an old truck to pass our way; they were heading north, trying to join the battle and stop you. Even though they already knew it was a losing battle."

"Stopping us?"

"Stopping the German tanks marching towards Paris." I have to imagine them, feel the story.

"We abandoned Dad's car that morning after it ran out of gas, and Mom allowed me to take only one suitcase, which I was already having a hard time carrying while sweating from the heat of the sun. We'd been walking for a few hours by the time they appeared above us."

"I'm listening."

"At first, they seemed like insignificant tiny dots in the sky to me; I looked up at the disturbing hum that overcame the noise of the cicadas in the fields, and saw them. Have you ever heard the sound of cicadas in the wheat fields in May and June?"

"No, never."

"There were four planes. Suddenly they changed course and dived on us, getting bigger by the second. We all ran away, screaming into the fields on the side of the road and scattering everywhere. The buzzing noise changed to a painful squealing of engines whirring, with the hammer's pounding of machine gun fire along the ruined road. Maybe they thought we were military men, maybe they were just coming back from a mission and were left with some ammunition, and didn't want to return it to base."

Philip is silent, sitting and watching me, and I go on talking.

"I never thought planes made such terrible noise." I must think about them, even though I'm trying not to.

"Yes, they make terrible noise."

"Then there was silence; only the noise of the bombs resounded

in my ears while I rose from the
ground, scratched by the weeds
I had flattened upon in the field.
I searched for Mom and Dad with
my eyes, among all the people who
stood up between the trampled
oats, but they didn't stand like all
the others. They just lay quietly
on the side of the road, in an
embrace. Dad had tried to protect
her with his body, wearing a white
shirt that now had a growing
bloodstain on his back, and Mom
lay with her face to the sky,
smiling at him, as if indifferent to
the red puddle coming out of her
back, painting the grey asphalt."
I see them in my imagination
while speaking slowly; what really
happened to them?

"I'm listening."

"But the people didn't care, they just got up and checked themselves, seeing if they were all right, returning to the road, keeping on strolling heading south. I still remember the pitying looks they gave me. Do you know what's the stupidest thing?"

"What?"

"All that time, what bothered me was that Mom would be mad at me for losing my suitcase when I ran from the planes into the field."

"And did you find the suitcase?"

"No, I just stood on the side of the road staring at them, not knowing what to do, while the whole convoy passed me in silence. Until one woman took pity on me and picked me up with her, bringing me to Paris to my aunt, with whom I live to this day."

"Now that was good enough, you've convinced me of your story. I hope you will persuade the German who might sit in front of you. It's important that you talk about your arrival in Paris and where you live. By the way, the tear you shed when you talked about your parents, it was good."

"See you next time." I get up from the wooden chair and head out, waiting to climb the stairs and exit the damp basement where we are meeting.

"See you next time. And try to get more information."

I have known him for almost a year now, meeting with him about once a month. And for almost a year now, he has been examining me, making sure I do not fail, and for almost a year now, he is not happy with me.

At least I'm not Jewish anymore. I'm Monique Otin, who lives in the 8th arrondissement, working in a boulangerie on the boulevard next to the opera.

***

"You're late." Simone, the boulangerie owner, scolds me as I quietly enter the next morning, closing the glass door behind me.

"I apologize, Mrs. Simone."

"Hurry up; your kingdom is waiting for you."

"Good morning." I hang my bag on the hanger and smile at Claudine, the second employee, who stands behind the counter.

"Good morning, how are you?"

"Monique, the tools in the back are waiting just for you."

"I'm going there, Mrs. Simone."

I quickly tie the white apron around my waist and rush into my kingdom in the back room, near Chef Martin. Here I spend my time washing dishes and cleaning the floor, sometimes I help Martin knead the dough, but usually I devoutly scrub the large baking pans.

From time to time, I have to go out among the customers, move a cloth around on the floor and wipe baguette and croissant crumbs off the seating tables. While working quietly, I listen to the buyers' conversation, keeping my head down.

"If you're done washing the baking pans, help Martin arrange the stock in the pantry, and then help Claudine clean the tables."

"Yes, Mrs. Simone." I wipe the sweat off my forehead and get up from the little wooden chair in the corner, going to the pantry to help Martin.

There is fine butter on our shelves, and there is no shortage of flour, cinnamon, or any other ingredient that would prevent Martin from baking. Even real chocolate arrives once a week, unloaded from a special truck approved by the authorities. We have everything needed to please the German soldiers during their stay in Paris, or as Simone calls them, 'our happy German customers.' A crispy morning baguette on the way to the Headquarters at Rue Rivoli, fragrant croissants to bring to a commander's meeting, and in the evenings, a slice of chocolate cake to the mistress waiting in her apartment.

Porcelain trays display Martin's masterpieces, protected by showcase glass and sold by Claudine's smile, all for German Reichsmarks or Vichy government francs. Every coin is welcomed in Simone's outstretched hand, quickly entering the cash register with a cheerful ring. We can be happy; after all, we are a favorite Nazi boulangerie in the heart of the Headquarters area.

"Take a break; I'll manage on my own." Martin expels me from his kingdom, but I stay, handing him the sack of flour. Even though it's my job to go out among them, it's hard for me to listen to the German soldiers in the boulangerie.

"Go, Claudine needs you."

The boulangerie is full of soldiers in green-grey uniforms; they stand patiently in line, laughing with each other and filling the small space with cigarette smoke and the odor of male sweat.

"Shall we go for a walk at the end of the day?" Claudine asks me as she takes an order from a German officer, flirting with him with her eyes.

"Yes, of course."

"Three and a half Reichsmarks." She reaches out her hand to him, and he puts the money in her palm, holding her fingers for a moment as if inviting her to a prom dance.

"Thank you very much. Come again." Her smile is dedicated especially to him.

She always looks perfect with her wavy black hair, just like the latest fashion. Sometimes she even puts on lipstick, ignoring Simone's remarks about it being inappropriate.

"Who's next? Monique, help me."

"And what's the name of the young frau?" A fair-haired soldier turns to me, and I look down, having a hard time looking at his uniform and staying calm.

"He is waiting for you," Claudine whispers to me as she lowers her voice and turns to serve a

handsome pilot wearing dark grey
uniforms.

***

"I saw you were excited about
him." Claudine teases me after
we say goodbye to Simone and
Martin, starting our walk down the
boulevard towards the Opera metro
station.

"I saw you were excited about the
pilot."

"He was flirty. I think he is a fighter
pilot."

"How do you know he's a fighter
pilot?"

"All fighter pilots are sure of
themselves, and he also has a lot
of medals of honor, probably for

shooting down enemy aircraft.
Not many like him arrive at the
boulangerie."

"And what did he say to you?"

"He said that I have beautiful eyes
and that I should go out with him."

"And will you?"

The exit of the metro, at Place de
l'Étoile, is packed with German
soldiers who have come to see
the world-famous boulevard, and
I cringe in the aisle, careful not to
rub against them.

"Monique, you are not listening to
me."

"Sorry, what did you answer?"

"I told him I don't know him at all
and that I can't go out with him."

"And that's it? Did he give up?"

"No, not at all, I told you he is sure of himself."

"So how did it end?"

"He said he would return to Le Bourget, they have a Messerschmitt squadron there, but he will come again tomorrow."

"And will you go out with him?"

"I don't know."

"Doesn't it bother you, going out with a German officer?"

"At least he will treat me politely and take me out, not like all the French men, talking all the time about how difficult life in Paris is these days."

"I wouldn't be able to go out with a German soldier."

"Maybe we should go out together, me with my pilot, and you with the one who wanted to talk to you."

"He didn't like me at all."

"He does, you'll see he will come tomorrow, he's interested in your beauty, you just have to start wearing makeup."

"How do you know he is interested?"

"Because I have experience with that sort of thing."

"But I'm not pretty."

"Believe me; you are, I know about this." And she folds her arm in mine as we walk down the Champs Elysees, watching the café full of German soldiers and their girls.

I never thought I was beautiful.

How beautiful could I feel if, from the day my breasts started to grow, everyone looked at the yellow badge stuck on my chest? How attractive could I feel in the simple dress Mom bought me? Or in that old coat I was wearing, trying to become as invisible as I could?

"The worst thing is getting noticed," Mom had explained to me, firmly refusing to have my hair permed as I'd seen in the glittering posters of movie stars hanging on the billboards in the street. "Worst of all is drawing the attention of a policeman or a soldier." She yelled at me when she discovered the magazine with the pictures I had tried to hide.

"You will never dress like those whores." She ripped it apart and threw the pages into the fireplace, replacement for the heating logs we were so desperate for.

"I'm sorry I was born into this family," I yelled at her in tears and ran to the dark stairwell, unable to see the torn magazine on fire.

But Claudine thinks I'm beautiful as we walk around the cafés, even though I do not have perfect wavy hair like hers.

"This soldier is also interested in going out with you." She squeezes my arm and laughs, pointing to a handsome armored soldier standing in his black uniform, watching us pass the boulevard, and I'm trying to smile. She must never know why I hold back from the German soldiers.

"Good night, see you tomorrow."

Claudine is walking to her home, and I'm heading to the apartment which has been my home for almost a year.

How would my life look if I was in her place instead of mine? I think as I pass the large billboard on the street. Would I be excited about hanging out with German soldiers? Or would I continue to worry every morning on my way to work?

***

"ID, please."

Just a few minutes' walk separates the quiet boulevard and the billboard with the worker's poster looking to the horizon and the guards' post in Concorde

Square, the checkpoint for the Headquarters area.

"Guten morgen." I hand the cardboard card to the guard, looking around as he examines it carefully. The barbed wire fences and wooden barriers are spread along the road, destroying the square's beauty. Why are they looking at my ID for so long? They should already know me by now. Did they notice my trembling fingers?

"Name?"

"Monique Otin, I passed here yesterday and the day before and the day before."

"Where are you going?"

"I work near the opera."

For almost a year now, I have been passing by the guard post every morning, and for almost a year now, I have to calm myself down as I approach the German soldiers standing near the barbed wire.

The sergeant looks at the ID for another moment, examining my face in front of the photograph as I look back at him until he relents, returning it to me.

"Have a nice day, Frau Otin." He taps his heels tightly and makes me cringe for a second as I return the ID to the leather bag resting on my shoulder.

"Have a nice day, Sergeant." I try to smile at him and continue walking down the street, looking at the senior officer's cars, parked in a straight line in front of the

building, under the huge red
Nazi flag that flies in the morning
breeze.

Keep going ahead, look down,
memorize the vehicle numbers,
count the guards at the
Headquarters entrance, and smile
at the bored drivers polishing their
officer's cars. I hope they engage
me in conversation and provide me
with some information along the
way, like last week when I learned
about the new division arriving in
France.

The quiet sound of the red flag
above my head makes me quicken
my steps, though I need to calm
down, must not arouse suspicion.
It moves calmly and serenely,
looking down at me, and I lower
my gaze, trying to avoid the black
swastika sewn in the center of

the white circle, just a few more minutes of tension.

The edge of the building is already approaching, my eyes examining several military trucks that pass through the street in slow motion, memorizing the unit symbol painted on their sides. In a few steps I'll turn to the avenue leading to the opera.

"Mademoiselle." I'm looking back to the soldier running towards me, and I stand still.

Breathe quietly, do not tremble, and do not run away; keep calm.

"Mademoiselle, the scarf, it fell from your bag." He catches up with me, all sweaty, handing it to me with a smile.

"Danke schön." I smile at him and

170

turn onto Opera Avenue, taking a deep breath and holding the leather bag tightly until my fingers turn white from the effort. In a few more minutes, Simone will ask me why I'm late again, and Claudine will ask if we will go for a walk together after work among the cafés on the boulevard.

"Not today," I will have to answer, "Today I cannot."

At the end of the day, the boy will probably be waiting for me next to the newsstand.

***

"I apologize, I have to go visit her mother today. I promised I'd do it after work."

"I thought we could take a walk down the boulevard." Claudine fails to hide her disappointment as we leave the boulangerie at the end of the day, walking arm in arm down the avenue. "She's always asking you for favors."

"I owe her, she let me sleep in her home, I cannot refuse her when she asks me to help her."

"Do you want me to join you?" She stops next to me at the newsstand.

"No thanks, you'll be bored."

My fingers search among the newspapers hanging on the walls of the stand. I pretend to look for a particular newspaper from the poor selection of wartime magazines, but my attention is on the boy with the grey casquette, the one standing with his back to me.

"The usual place," he whispers
to me as he loads a pack of
newspapers into a large leather
bag, continuing on his way, and
I do not answer him, hoping
Claudine did not hear his whisper.

"Why are you looking for a
newspaper? They're just full of war
stories anyway."

"She likes me to read to her. It's
already hard for her to read."

Claudine takes a magazine with a
red title and a photograph of a pilot
on the cover, handing it to me.

"Buy her the German Army
newspaper in Paris, the Signal; she
probably won't notice."

"Put it back; they'll think we intend
to buy it." I laugh at her.

"No one cares what we do." She waves the magazine in front of my face, but finally relents and returns it to the stand.

"Goodbye, I have to go, she's waiting for me, we'll meet tomorrow." I hug her quickly and walk away, holding one of the government newspapers in my hand. It announces a further reduction in meat rations. The man near the Metro Opera is waiting for me already.

Next to the billboard, I stop and look at a poster showing a new movie star in a red dress, taking the time to look over my shoulder. Is anyone following me? The soldier by the stairs is waiting for me, or has he made an appointment with another girl? And what about the café across the street? It's full of German soldiers, are they looking in my direction?

At a slow pace, I cross the avenue and approach the marble railing of the entrance to the metro, looking around and pretending I'm looking at the opera house which overlooks the boulevard, ignoring the red flags with swastikas hanging in front of it.

Nothing around looks suspicious. I can keep walking to the basement in the Latin Quarter, my meeting place with Philip.

***

He waits for me at the entrance to a basement in the Latin Quarter, standing at the bottom of the stairs, looking up as I descend towards him, and finally climbing a few steps in my direction. He's still wearing a simple white shirt with his sleeves rolled up below his elbows, his quiff still wild, and he still has a gun sticking out of his belt as he looks at me with his brown eyes, examining me.

"I've been waiting too long for you."

"I arrived as quickly as I could." I hold my head.

A small table and two chairs stand in the corner, but he does not offer me to sit, and we remain standing, facing each other as I look up at him.

"How is the underground? How is the revolution progressing?"

"We will win, but revolutions do not happen in a single day. What did you bring with you?"

"Not much."

He walks away from me, taking a few steps into the small basement as I follow him with my gaze.

"I can't get much information, the guards near the headquarters examine me all the time, and in the boulangerie I hardly walk around among the soldiers. Simone wants me to wash dishes all day."

For almost a year now, I have had the feeling that he is disappointed in me, sorry he had not found a more effective German speaker instead. One that would not be afraid of the German soldiers entering the boulangerie, or would be willing to go out with them.

They are walking like tourists all over the city, holding city maps supplied by the German army, looking for French girls to guide them through the wonders of the city of lights. But I'm not effective as he expected; in the end, he will get rid of me, leave me to my fate.

"There are some new senior officers' cars outside the headquarters, and I have new gossip from Claudine."

"Do you have the vehicle descriptions or numbers?" He approaches me again, takes a piece of paper and a pencil out of his pocket, but still does not ask me to sit down.

"Let me write the numbers for you."

"I'll write. If they catch me and

get to the paper, they must not recognize your handwriting."

"You were wrong here," I point out and correct him, touching his fingers by mistake and looking away in embarrassment, but continuing to tell him the numbers, ignoring the warmth of his touch.

He has the pleasant smell of a man mixed with the scent of a printing house, but I have to concentrate, trying to remember every piece of information, even the smallest ones, like what I heard from Claudine.

"She is now excited about a pilot stationed in Le Bourget."

"That's good. Maybe it will bring us more information." Why am I not like her?

"Don't you want to check my story, like last time?"

"Not today, I have to hurry. We'll continue to build your story next time."

"Will we meet next month?"

"Yes, we'll meet next month." He walks away from me again, turning around in the damp basement as if he already wants to get out of here, into the air outside. He is disappointed in me.

"Goodbye." I turn and head up the stairs.

"Monique," he takes my arm, stopping me.

"Yes?" I look up at him.

"Be careful."

"You too, take care." I release my hand and turn my back to him, climbing back onto the street. The man with the bike is waiting for me outside. He will escort me back to the city's east bank; from there, I will continue home by myself. Like always, at the end of the boulevard I will make a detour, avoiding the billboard with the huge poster.

For months now, "Come Work in Germany" has been glued to the giant billboard on the boulevard. The words are written in black square letters, and above them is a painting of a sturdy worker. In his hands, he holds a sledgehammer while his eyes look beyond the horizon. Maybe he knows something?

***

My footsteps in my simple shoes hit the avenue's pavement stones. It is too late, and I have to hurry home; it was a mistake to stop again in front of the billboard. My name is Monique Otin and not Monique who could not hug her parents goodbye. I have a new life, and I must not think about them, but maybe the painting on the billboard can give me some clue? The sledgehammer in his hand? The green fields behind him? The blue sky?

I raise my eyes as I approach the billboard and examine every detail closely. Who are the French men going to work in Germany? Why are they willing to work in factories and farms instead of all those recruited German soldiers? Could it be that the Germans took them too? Why haven't I heard from them for almost a year? Maybe the man painted in the poster knows? Perhaps he knows what happened to Mom and Dad and Jacob?

But the poster doesn't have a drawing of a barbed wire fence. Why did I let the train worker stop me a few months ago when I ran towards the fences? Why did I let him knock me down on the railway?

My hand wipes away the tears as I continue my way home. I shouldn't go near the billboard, and Lizette is probably waiting at home. At least I have someone taking care of me.

***

Lizette

My footsteps are barely heard
on the marble stairs as I quickly
ascend to the fifth floor, pull the
key out of the brown leather bag
Lizette bought me as a gift for my
eighteenth birthday, and quietly
open the white door.

"Shall I make us some coffee?" She
always asks me that when I walk
into her house and put the bag in
the entrance hall, even though it's
my job to serve her and not the
other way around.

"I will make some, you can
continue reading your book." But
she is already getting up and
walking to the kitchen with her
high-stepping walk.

"You worked all day; it's good for me to do something."

As we wait for the water to boil, I look at her hair, which has started to turn silver, and at her hands, gently holding the porcelain cups while placing them on the silver tray.

"You were late. I'd already started worrying about you."

"Simone delayed me at work, sometimes she asks me to stay, and I have to."

"Did you cry?"

"I have to learn not to take the things she says to heart."

"Shall we sit in the living room?" She holds the kettle in her manicured hands and pours the boiling water carefully. "I got some sugar, one teaspoon can make life much sweeter, and also improve the taste of this disgusting coffee." She smiles at me as she places the glasses on the tray while the silver bracelets on her wrists rattle, making me remember the first time we met, almost a year ago.

"Lizette, this is Monique Otin, she's going to help you with the apartment, just like you asked." The woman who'd brought me introduced me to the impressive woman standing at the door of the fancy apartment. She examined me, and I lowered my eyes and looked at my torn shoes. Lizette looked a little older than Mom, and her hair was starting to turn white at the edges, which added charm and splendor to her appearance. Her dress was a lovely mustard color, and she wore new leather shoes, not a cheap wartime imitation like I had. I was ashamed to stand in front of her like that, with my old grey dress, and all my belongings packed under my arm in a paper bag, one more used dress and a pair of underwear given to me by the woman who accompanied me, whose name I did not even know.

"Nice to meet you," Lizette shook my hand cordially, inviting me in. "I'll show you to your room."

With her hand on my waist, she soothed my fears, accompanying me up the stairs to the attic, my new home, not before saying goodbye to my companion who then disappeared into the darkness.

And just like that, my new life
started. Every morning I assist
this impressive lady with the
management and cleaning of her
apartment, and in return, she
gives me a place to stay. Soon
after finishing the housework,
I will hurry to my second job in
the boulangerie as a dishwasher,
beneath Simone's comments. But
Lizette always treats me right.
"Your help is important to me," she
tells me every time she buys me
a new dress or jacket, and most
of the time I think that it's not
the need for help that caused her
to let me into her house, but her
loneliness.

She places the silver tray on the
table in the living room as I sit
down in front of her and wait
patiently; her peaceful movements
relax me.

"So what happened that you got back so late?"

"Simone is disappointed in me."

She must not know about my double life; I will never be able to tell her.

"Why do you think she is disappointed in you?"

"She expects me to be more efficient, and I am not."

"Maybe you misinterpret her behavior?"

"It does not seem so; she always asks me questions and hurries away from me at the end of the day."

"What we feel is not always what they think; it takes time to get to know people."

I lean back and look around the elegant room, staring at the picture in the silver frame, the one standing on the mantle in the living room, as I sip my bitter coffee.

"It also took a long time for you before you knew?"

"No, I knew from the first moment, but I'm just an old woman, you do not have to listen to me," she smiles at me. "At my age, you don't want to change the world anymore, you just think about the small things in life, like adding a teaspoon of sugar to terrible coffee."

Lizette is right; I have a place to sleep, food in my stomach, and Claudine as a friend to walk with after work, that should be more than enough for my new life.

"Let's go to sleep; tomorrow is a new day." She smiles at me, and I head up the stairs to the attic. Tomorrow is a new day.

***

The Champs Elysees is quiet in the early morning hours as I walk down the boulevard on my way to work. The car traffic is sparse due to the lack of fuel, and the wide road seems too big for the few vehicles that pass through it from time to time. A military truck full of soldiers passes by, its tires making noise on the rough road, and it leaves behind a sharp smell of burnt fuel and a greyish cloud as it heads to the Concorde Square barricaded by barbed wire fences.

The gazes of the soldiers in the truck make me back away from the road to the safety of the cafés, walking between the empty chairs.

"Coffee, mademoiselle?" asks a bored waiter standing at the entrance, looking at me as if trying to remember whether we'd already met.

"No, thanks." I continue walking. I was delayed this morning in arranging the house, and I must hurry. At such hours they do not serve real coffee to the French people on their way to work. The espresso machines pour a leaky liquid made from ground beans, which were browned and called "coffee substitute" by the waiters even though it doesn't taste like coffee at all. The fragrant coffee bags that come by special delivery will only be opened in the afternoon, especially for the customers who wear grey-green uniforms and those willing to get acquainted with them.

"Mademoiselle, can you take a photo of us?" I am asked by two German soldiers standing on the boulevard and holding a camera. I pretend not to hear them and speed up my steps, Claudine would've known what to answer them.

***

"Did you see how he looked at you?" Claudine whispers to me, pointing towards a young man who passes us and smiles at her while we walk hand in hand, enjoying the afternoon sun.

"He looked at you, not me."

"Of course not, he wants to invite you for a walk with him."

We both walk up the Champs Elysees, looking at the cafés full of German soldiers and their French girls. Claudine critiques their dresses, and I examine the men's uniforms, memorizing their rank insignia.

"You need to smile more often; you're so serious."

"But it's embarrassing to smile."

"You are wrong, it's fun, and besides that, you have a nice smile. Do you see the guy standing by the café? Smile at him and lower your gaze, signal to him that you like him, but he has to make the first move."

"But he's looking at you."

"He is looking at us, and he is interested in you, in you and your beauty."

"How do you know?"

"I already told you, I have experience in men's gazes."

"How's your flirty pilot?"

"He came in today and invited me out. Even Simone smiled at him after she saw how many cookies he bought."

"And will you go out with him?"

"Look at her." Claudine stops, pointing with her head at one of the fancy cafés on the boulevard, my eyes following her.

"Who is she?"

"She's a famous movie star."

The famous movie star is wearing a fashionable long red dress, sitting in the café, laughing gracefully. She holds a white cigarette with a perfect hand covered in a black glove, surrounded by several high-ranking German officers, shining in their neat uniforms and medals.

"Who is she?"

"Her name is Arletty, but you don't go to the movies anyway, so you will not know her."

More passersby stop and look out the café windows, but some look away and spit on the pavement while walking on.

"Let's go on; it's unpleasant here."

"It seems to me that everyone is in love with her."

"How can that be?"

"Because she's so special."

"And how do you know you're in love?"

"You feel it, all over your body, you're hot, and you get excited when you know you'll meet him soon."

"And it's nice?"

"It's a little stressful, but it's also pleasant, like when you walk together, and you let him hold your hand, feeling the warmth of his palm, or when he hugs you, and sometimes even more."

"And what's that 'even more'?"

"Monique, Monique Moreno?" I hear a call and turn my head.

"I'm Monique, but Monique Otin, not Moreno," I answer the young man who approaches us, feeling a cold wave pass through my whole body.

"Monique Moreno? Don't you remember me? Jean, Jean Bosse, I studied with you in school."

"Sorry, I do not remember you, we're in a hurry."

"Monique, how are you? How are you surviving the war with all the restrictions?"

"I'm sorry, we have to go." I grab Claudine's arm and pull her towards the road, wanting to cross the avenue to the other side.

"Who is he? What happened to you? You're hurting me."

"Sorry, I did not mean to."

"Who is he? Why did he call you Moreno?"

"He was confused by the name. I hated him at school. He used to hit me."

"Isn't Moreno a Jewish name?" Claudine lowers her voice, getting closer to my ear.

"I have no idea. I hated him. What about your pilot? You didn't tell me the end of the story."

"Are you Jewish?" She stops and looks at me, releasing our hands.

"No, I'm not Jewish, I hate Jews, I told you he had me confused for some other Monique."

Is he following us? I must not look; I must act as if nothing has happened. I am not a Jew; I have never been a Jew.

"Will you go out with your handsome pilot?"

"What about the woman you are living with? Does Lizette know?"

"I already told you, I'm not Jewish; he was confused." I must keep going as if nothing had happened.

"Monique, wait," Claudine catches up with me and grabs my arm again. "It's okay, I promise not to tell, it's a secret between us."

"There is no secret, I am not Jewish, and you should continue telling me about the pilot." I grab her arm and look at the German soldiers in the cafés; they look more threatening.

"Obviously you're not Jewish, just stay away from my wallet." She laughs and continues to hold my arm as we stroll down the avenue. I keep on smiling and behave as if nothing has happened, but my heart is racing now. Why is this happening to me? Why did he suddenly appear? Will she tell anyone else?

"You promised to tell me about the pilot."

"The pilot? The pilot wants to go out with me; most of all, I like that he has no big nose and that he is not stinky." She continues to walk with a cheerful look while holding my arm.

I must keep ignoring her, let her forget, it did not happen.

***

Philip is waiting for me at the bottom of the stairs, and I can already smell the damp basement; what shall I tell him about Claudine? For days I've been trying to decide what to say to him, especially since Simone started looking at me differently. But when I asked Claudine, she swore to me that she had told her nothing.

How will he react if I tell him? How angry will he be? I have to go down the stairs.

"I arrived as quickly as I could." I'm smiling at him, trying to hide my anxiety.

"I've been waiting too long for you." He smiles, keeps standing too close.

"Shall we sit down?" I offer, and he pulls away.

But even when he sits at the other side of the small table, his eyes make me nervous.

"What happened?"

"Everything is fine."

"Are you sure?"

"There are a lot more German soldiers in the boulangerie, and Claudine wants to go out with the pilot. She keeps talking about him."

"What is she saying?"

"That he is a fighter pilot in the Messerschmitt squadron, located at Le Bourget airfield. He was previously stationed in North Africa. A lot of new units are coming from North Africa these days, and she may suspect that I am Jewish."

"What does that mean?"

"His entire squadron was transferred to Le Bourget after the German withdrawal from North Africa."

"I did not mean that."

"So what did you mean?"

"What did you said about Claudine?"

"She may suspect me of being Jewish."

"How did that happen?" The creaking of the chair on the basement's stone floor is jarring to my ears as Philip gets up from his chair and stands up, his hands leaning on the table.

"We walked down the boulevard, and she said something against the

Jews, adding that I look like a Jew, and I didn't deny it fast enough."

"Is that all?"

"It seems to me she thinks I'm a Jew, even though I denied it."

"Was that all?" He walks away from the table and turns his back to me, but after a moment he returns and watches me, as if I'd disappointed him again.

"Yeah, that's all it was." I also stand up and put my hands on the table. "She probably realized I'm a Jew and she's gossipy, that's Claudine. She's also my friend."

"She's not your friend; she's Monique Otin's friend." He puts his hands on my palms and brings his face closer. "And she likes to talk." His scent is strong to me.

"I know she likes to talk. All the information you get from me comes from her mouth because she likes to talk." I release my hands and stand still, looking up at him. The main thing is not to look down, so he doesn't notice I am afraid of him.

"Okay," he calms down and sits, looking at me with a look of disappointment, "we'll see what to do with her."

"Okay." I also sit down and continue to report everything I know to him, lowering my eyes and concentrating on his fingers on the table, thinking how it felt to touch them the last time we'd met.

"Take care of yourself," he tells me as we say goodbye.

"Do not worry about Claudine," I

say goodbye to him, and touch his palm for a moment. "She will not speak."

But in the days to come, she never stops laughing at my big nose, even though my nose is small.

***

Claudine

"Monique, I need you," Claudine calls out through the hustle and bustle of noon, and I leave the baking pan I'm cleaning in the back room, wiping my hands and walking over to her.

"Yes?"

"Please take care of these two gentlemen." And I freeze in my place.

The Boulangerie space is full as usual, with German soldiers filling up the room with German jokes mixed with cigarette smoke, but my attention is on the two men standing in front of me. They do not wear uniforms, but long leather coats as they stand by the counter, waiting just for me.

"Yes, please?"

"Are you Monique?" The shorter of the two asks me, in good French.

"Yes." For a moment, I get confused while the tall one looks at me.

"Can you help us?" My fingers start shaking.

"Yes, please?"

"May we have two butter croissants and two chocolate croissants, please?"

"How did you know my name?"

"From your friend, she called you and told us." The tall one smiles at me, causing me to shiver.

After they leave and the glass
door slams behind them, I
escape to the back room, unable
to stop scrubbing the baking
pans forcefully, even though the
boulangerie is still full of soldiers
and Simone asks me several times
to go out and help. What will I tell
Philip the next time we meet?

"What happened to your fingers?"
A few days later, I sit down in front
of him in the basement, placing my
hands on the old wooden table.

His hand tries to grab my scratched
fingers and examine them, but I
hurry to remove my hands from
the table, placing them in my lap.

"What happened to your hand?" I
look at his hand on the table.

"It's nothing." His palm is wrapped with a dirty bandage, and I notice the bloodstain.

"How did it happen?"

"It's not serious, how are you? What happened to your fingers?"

"It's just scratches. Does your hand hurt?"

"It's a pain, but it looks a lot worse than it is. What information did you bring with you?"

"Not much."

On my way back to the east bank, I wonder if I did right by not telling him about the two strangers in the long leather coats, or that every night, when Claudine and I part, she calls me Monique Moreno with a smile. Should I have told him?

It's probably just my imagination which makes me so tense.

***

"Let's go to a different place, let's go to Husman Avenue." Claudine tries to persuade me to join her on an evening walk, while we both wait for Martin to lock the bakery's iron back door.

"I don't know." I'm afraid to deviate from our routine.

"Come on, let's do something different; the evenings are warmer, and maybe there are new clothes in the storefronts." She goes on, and I don't want to tell her that I have no clothing ration tickets, nor money to buy what the shops on the boulevard have to offer.

"I don't like the spring fashion; it's boring."

"This whole war is boring. I wish it were all over." But she gives up, and we are heading on our way down the avenue, walking side by side.

"Maybe you should think again about going with a German officer?" she asks me as several soldiers pass by and stare at us.

"I don't think I could do that."

"The pilot won't give up; he keeps inviting me, and not just him. They are so impressive in their medal-decorated uniforms."

But my attention is given to the newsstand and the boy leaning in the corner. He is hanging the newspapers in his usual way, even though only a few days have passed since my last meeting with Philip.

"What did you say?"

"That they are very polite when they invite me out, even when I refuse."

"But they are our occupiers; they can decide when to be polite and when to behave less politely."

"You don't have to be afraid of them; no one can guess about you, even though your nose might cause a big problem." She takes my hand and laughs.

I know she doesn't mean to hurt me, but I don't know how to make her stop; anyway, I have to go now, the kid at the newsstand is waiting for me.

"I'm sorry, I completely forgot, I promised Lizette that I would help her."

"Don't you get tired of her asking things from you? You should stand on your own," she complains when we kiss goodbye.

"I have no choice; I owe her." I kiss Claudine on both cheeks and turn around, heading to the newsstand.

My eyes search for the boy at the back of the newsstand, but he is not there. The newspapers hanging outside are lined up perfectly, the man inside the stand is sitting sleepily, and as much as I look around and down the street, I can't see him.

"Two newspapers, please." It's a sign of danger, my hands are shaking while I'm paying the man.

"Mademoiselle, you took one or two newspapers?"

"Two." Why is there a dark vehicle standing in the corner?

"You paid me only for one."

"Sorry, I apologize," I hand him more money. "Where is the boy?"

"Which boy?"

"The kid who's always in the back here, arranging the newspapers."

"Theirs is no kid here; I'm here alone."

"Never mind."

"Are you okay?"

Stay calm, stroll down the avenue. How come the vendor at the newsstand doesn't know the kid? Carefully examine all the passersby. Why are they looking in my direction? Do not stop walking, has there been something unusual lately?

Where's Claudine? I must find her; we'll keep on walking together as if nothing happened. I'll tell her I got confused and that we can continue strolling down the avenue.

The man with the long coat, have I seen him before? What does he have in the suitcase he is carrying in his left hand? And the young man in the corner standing next to his bike, why is he looking in my direction? Who are the two people running towards the crowd gathered at the end of the street? What is going on there?

I must keep walking as if nothing

has happened, cross the street to the other side. All the people are crowded around something, a few of them are kneeling on the sidewalk. A woman is lying in the road, wearing low-heeled cream-colored shoes; Claudine has low-heeled cream-colored shoes.

"A vehicle passed at high speed and hit her," a woman in a greenish scarf speaks excitedly as she describes what happened to the policeman while he writes down her words in his notepad. "He did not stop at all, luckily I noticed he was approaching, he almost hit and killed me too."

As I get closer to her, I must use my hands to push myself through all the people surrounding her, moving them by force. Carefully I lean over the hard asphalt, ignoring the policeman's request not to gather and not listening to all the talking above my head.

Someone put a coat under her head, and someone tried to arrange her hand, which is lying at an unnatural angle, but it does not seem to bother her anymore. Her eyes remain open to the sky with a look of misunderstanding, and through my tears I see a man's hand reaching to her eyes, slowly lowering her eyelids.

***

The painted figures from the New Testament watch me from the church ceiling with an inquisitive gaze, as I raise my head and study them. While trying to identify their names, I wonder if they will start shouting that I do not belong here, nor does the simple coffin painted with dark varnish and placed in front of me.

I have no idea how I got home that day, whether on the metro or by foot, crying and stumbling on the pavements shaking under my feet. I do not even remember if it started to rain or if there was a chilly evening breeze. The only thing I couldn't forget were the sirens of the approaching ambulance, and the policeman cried out: "Do not gather, anyone who has seen how this happened will approach me, all the rest, please leave."

Churches scares me; at least this one doesn't have threatening demons like in the Notre Dame

Cathedral. Demons screaming at me from above that it's my fault she's dead.

Because of me, we did not go around the shops as she wanted, because of me we delayed those few seconds when we parted on the sidewalk, and I went to look for the child near the newsstand. If I had only accepted her offer, none of this would have happened. We would have left the boulangerie by now, waiting for Martin to lock the back door and strolling hand in hand, like every day.

"You are to blame," the nightmares had shouted at me last night, waking me up with screams of black bats biting me and hurting my body.

Few people came to the ceremony,

and the church is almost empty, befitting days of war and scarcity. Some women in black, some hunchbacked old men holding walking sticks made of decorated wood, Simone who smiles at me even though everything happened because of me, Martin the chef, dignified without his white apron, and that's it. Not a single man that loved her, not a single man she loved. Not even the pilot arrived, nor any of those soldiers in grey-green uniforms, the ones who would chat with her in a very polite way. They must be wondering why the glass door is locked today, and they cannot enjoy the pleasures of the French capital, crispy croissants, and a woman behind the counter to flirt with.

"They don't know who the driver was," Simone is whispering to me.

"A policeman came this morning and informed me that they don't have the car number." She is trying to hug me. "It's such a pity; she was a lovely girl."

"I am so sorry," I say voicelessly to the simple coffin in front of me, looking up at the ceiling paintings of Jesus and the Virgin. Maybe they will forgive me for not walking with her down the avenue, as she'd asked.

"Monique, come and help me for a moment." I hear Simone's call in the back room.

"I'll be right there." My fingers place the baking pan in the sink, and I'm wiping my hands, hurrying to help her serve the German soldiers.

"Go, I'll wash it," Martin offers to help. Since Claudine died, everyone has tried to treat me more nicely, even Simone. But her expressions of affection seem to me like a wolf dog's attempts to restrain herself from a passing rabbit, making me wonder when she will not be able to hold back and return to scolding me.

Where is the boy? Why did he disappear that day?

Although I'm not supposed to stop at the newsstand, I can't resist myself. My fingers run across the line of German army magazines, showing a picture of a new airplane on the cover, while I'm pretending to concentrate on the photography and looking around for the boy. Why has he not been there since? I can't ask the seller.

"May I help you?" he asks, waking up from his sleepy gaze.

"Do you have cigarettes?"

"Do you know that according to government regulations, women are not allowed to smoke?"

"Yes, it's not for me."

"Counterfeit?" He lowers his voice.

"No."

"The real ones are very expensive."

"How much?"

"25 francs."

I take the imaginary sum out of my wallet and put it in his palm. With a swift motion, he puts a blue pack in my hand, taken out of some hiding place, returning to his indifferent stance at the stand.

I have nothing to do with those cigarettes, and I hold the box in my hand, intending to throw it into the nearest bin. But I change my mind at the last second and push it deep into my bag, maybe one day I will use them. The people who pass me look curiously at the young woman standing in the street, wiping her face with her hand.

"Can I offer you a handkerchief?" I hear a man's voice and look up.

"No thanks." I continue on my way, walking around the street corner where I last saw her, I can't return to that place.

The cafés on the Champs Elysees are still full of soldiers and their girlfriends, and I stand as far away as I can, trying not to hear the talking and the laughing around the tables. If some stranger calls my name, I will ignore him this time. Those two women walking ahead laughing remind me of the both of us. I cannot stand the avenue anymore; I have to get out of here.

Finally, I find the entrance to the metro, stepping down into the tunnel. The metro's darkness will embrace me, an escape from the cafés and the street.

Standing in the corner of the dim platform, I can examine the coming train, searching for the right car to get into, but a gang of running German soldiers arrives and push their way in just before the doors close.

"Mademoiselle, will you show me the city?"

"Mademoiselle, choose me. I am much more handsome. Nice to meet you, Max." He reaches out a hand.

"Don't choose him; Max replaces his girls all the time. You should choose me." Another soldier is reaching out.

But I lower my eyes, staring at my leather shoes, the ones that Lizette bought me, trying to avoid looking at their leather hobnail boots.

"She's a spoiled impolite Frenchwoman who doesn't like talking to handsome German soldiers," I hear one of them say to his friends in German. "She should thank us for saving her from Stalin's clutches. If we weren't here, she'd be speaking Russian by now." He keeps on talking, while my head is down and I say nothing, watching their hobnail boots getting closer. But finally they get away from the spoiled impolite French girl, walking to the other side of the metro car.

The creaking sound of the metro on the railway breaks the silence, while the rest of the people in the carriage watch me and say nothing, a dark grey mass of people who stood back and watched the German soldiers harass me and did nothing. My hand holds the metal rod tightly for support, and my fingers are becoming white from the effort. "Trocadéro," the white sign at the station appears, I have to get off.

At the platform, I stop for a moment, letting all the German soldiers get out of the metro car and go on their way outside, trying to avoid being crowded among them. I can still smell their tobacco on my way out, and hear them in the distance. The breeze in the corridor allows me to breathe, but when I go up the stairs into the square, they are all over me again.

The surface is crowded with soldiers, walking as tourists of victory, talking loudly and waving. Some of them are holding a camera or a Parisian girl, taking pride in their new purchase during a short stay in the city of pleasure.

I turn my gaze away from them, unable to watch their uniforms and the swastika flag stuck at the top of the Eiffel Tower, and I approach the older woman standing at the corner of the square. She is wearing a dirty coat and stands hunched, selling flowers to the soldiers and their girlfriends.

"How much will a flower cost me?"

"For you, it's free, my girl." But I insist on paying her.

"May a loving man give you a flower," the older woman whispers to me as she hands me the flower and receives the coin, holding it carefully in her wrinkled fingers.

"Don't cry, my girl, he will arrive one day." And I'm fighting the urge to hug her, turning my back and walking away.

The small cemetery is hidden behind the high wall overlooking the square, and it takes time for me to find the narrow entrance gate. I walk along the break in the wall until my eyes notice the small metal gate that creaks open under my hand. But I remember how to find the fresh grave. My steps slow down as I approach, placing the flower on the marble headstone.

"This is for you, my girl, may a loving man give a flower to you," my lips whisper to her when I sit down next to her.

"You know, Simone treats me much nicer, even though it's clear she prefers you to me." I smile at the letters engraved in the stone.

"And your pilot doesn't come anymore, at least I haven't seen him, but the boulangerie is always full of new soldiers, surely you could find someone else to invite you for a walk on the boulevard, buying you mint ice cream." I dry my tears slowly.

"There are many new armored and engineering soldiers in town. I have to memorize their unit numbers; it's for Philip. You do not know him yet; I promise to tell you about him the next time we meet." But the boy from the newsstand, I don't have the courage to tell her about him.

Before I say goodbye, I promise to visit again as soon as I can, heading to the small cemetery gate and on my way home, to Lizette.

But even the night talks with Lizette don't help. Time after time, I almost slip when I try to explain to her why I left Claudine in the street, looking for reasons and finally going silent. She must never know what happened that day, but the thoughts do not stop, making me feel so guilty. It

did not happen because of me.
It happened because of the boy
who'd disappeared. It happened
because the driver ran her over;
it happened because Simone
delayed us for a few minutes in the
boulangerie before we left.

***

"Good morning."

"Good morning, Monique, this is
Marie; she's going to replace you
at the dishes. From now on, you'll
work with me behind the counter."
And I stop for a moment at the
entrance, leaning on the glass door
and watching the very excited new
girl who is standing still.

"Nice to meet you." I shake her

hand and take her to the back room, guiding her through the list of chores that have been my responsibility until now, and finally handing her the old apron used for washing the baking pans, taking the clean white one from the hanger. The one that has been hanging around for days, waiting for Claudine.

"Do you need help?" Marie asks.

"No thanks, I'm fine." My fingers get mixed up tying the apron as I turn my back to her, I don't want her to ask about my eyes.

 The soldiers keep coming, running from the rainy street into the warm space, filling it with German language and the strong cigarette smoke of poor-quality tobacco. They laugh at each other while the

doorbell rings again and again as
it opens and closes, making me
tense. Many of them pay in silence
and walk away, just glancing
at me, but there are the more
daring ones who try to start a
conversation, practicing their poor
French while I keep quiet and lower
my head, not answering them.

Ranks, I need to look at their
ranks, memorize them. Also
unit tags, I should learn to
recognize their tags. What about
the red stripes sewn on some of
the soldiers' pants? What does
it mean? Should I start up a
conversation with them? That's
what Phillip expects me to do.

Occasionally, when there are fewer
soldiers in the boulangerie, I go to
the back room, looking for excuses
to watch Marie, but mostly looking

for a quiet moment to myself away from the doorbell noises and the German words in my ears.

Soon the end of the day will come, and I'll visit her and buy her a flower instead of a loving man. But on my way to the metro, when I pass the newsstand, I see the boy standing with his back to me.

"The usual place." I hear his whisper before he disappears, not stopping to provide me some explanation about what happened last time, and I'm standing and watching him walk away. I must hurry, Philip will tell me what happened, he will calm me down.

***

Philip's silhouette looks to me like a dark shadow waiting for me in the dim light of the basement lamp, but I know he is just protecting the entrance, making it safe for me.

"I've been waiting too long for you." He is still leaning against the damp wall, and I go down one more step, getting closer.

"I arrived as quickly as I could. How is your hand?" My fingers caress his hand, examining the wound in his palm, refusing to let go.

"I'll be fine, shall we sit down?" He gets away from me.

"Let's sit down."

"Everything is okay?"

My hands grip his body as my head

searches for a place to rest for a
moment under his enfolding arms,
and tears begin to flow from my
eyes. I know he is disappointed
with me, but I can't hold back
anymore; I need to tell him all
about her.

"What happened?" I feel the
warmth of his arms around me.

"It's Claudine." I start sobbing
and hug his body more tightly.
His fingers gently caress my hair,
smelling of gun oil mixed with
printing colors and his pleasant
scent.

"She is dead." The tears flow
with all the words that have
been waiting for so long. Without
stopping I tell him about the
accident and all the people
gathering around; I even tell him

about the coat under her head and her shoe, which remained on the street after the ambulance left.

"I wanted to pick up the shoe, out of some illogical thought that she might need it, but I just couldn't and kept going. And the next morning, as I passed and looked from a distance at the street corner, the shoe was gone." I can't stop crying under his caressing fingers.

"The rain washed the blood off the street, and passersby kept walking down the street, not stopping and thinking about the woman who lay there yesterday." I'm sobbing.

"Shhh…" He gently strokes my hair.

"And I was in church, and I apologized to all the angels who are guarding her from now on, and they forgave me, and Simone brought Marie to replace me with the dishwashing, and now I'm behind the counter instead of Claudine, having a hard time with all the German soldiers."

"Shhh... everything's fine." He continues to caress my hair while I hug him, trying to relax in the warmth of his pleasant body and hands that encircle me.

"And now you'll be happier with me." The tears do not stop.

"Shhh... it doesn't matter... what about the driver, did they catch him?"

"No, a policeman came to the boulangerie, saying they don't know who it was. What happened to the boy? Why did he disappear that day?"

"He had to get away, so he disappeared."

And I keep telling him about the soldiers coming in, entering the boulangerie and ordering their pastries, asking for his guidance on ranks and tags, because now I'm exposed to a lot more.

But suddenly, while I'm talking about my new place behind the counter, I have a terrible thought about that day, and even though I keep reporting everything I heard to him, that thought doesn't leave me. Like an ambulance siren, it rings in my mind, and slowly my speech slows until I fall silent.

"Shhhh... everything's fine." He continues stroking me, but I push his body away and look into his eyes, examining him through my tears.

"Why wasn't the boy there?"

"Because he had to go."

"The boy's disappearance is related to Claudine?"

"The boy's appearance is related to you; the boy is not related to Claudine."

"But I left her, and someone ran her over."

"It has nothing to do with you."

"How did you know the police haven't found the driver? I did not tell you about that." I try to get up off the floor and stand.

"It's not your business how I knew." He also gets up and walks away from me, watching me with his brown eyes.

"Did you run Claudine over?" I raise my voice.

"No, we did not run Claudine over."

"Did you kill Claudine because she exposed me? Please tell me you didn't kill her." I shout as I grab the wooden chair, supporting myself.

"No, we didn't." It takes him a while to answer me.

"What do you mean, you didn't? Who killed her?" The noise of the chair falling to the floor sounded like it was shattering on the concrete.

"Answer me, please, who ran her over?"

"It's not us."

"Please tell me, who did this to her?" My hands are holding the

244

table, keeping me from falling on the floor again.

"Someone else did it."

"Who is the someone else? Please, you must tell me."

"The Communist underground did it."

"But why? Why did they do that to her?" My tears flow down my cheeks as I look at the wall, examining the dark moss stains. I cannot look at him.

"Because we asked them for help." I hear his tired voice, as though coming from a distant place.

"But why?" I ask, again and again, knowing the answer in my heart but unable to stop, wanting to hear it in his own words.

"Because that's how it works,
they are fighting the Germans,
and we are fighting the Germans,
and because we have a common
enemy, we have common goals."

"But why kill her?"

"Because she endangered you and
us with her big mouth." He tries
to stay calm and get closer to me
again, but I walk away, looking at
the dirty wall.

"She wouldn't have spoken." My
fingers scratch the wall, peeling off
the plaster.

"If she hadn't said something
yet, it was only a matter of time
before she started to talk, and the
Germans would find out all about
you. Do you want to find yourself
in the basement of the house on 84
Avenue Foch?" He tries to control

his voice, but he sounds so distant to me.

"And what about me? Will you kill me too? If I'm not good enough?" I'm having a hard time breathing.

"You are one of us, and there is a reason why we accepted you." He tries to lower his voice and bring his hands close to me again for a hug, but I stop him with my hands, feeling the rough wall at my back.

"Just as long as I bring you what you want?"

"You are one of us; she wasn't. She was the one who wanted to go out with German soldiers, to lick their boots, do you remember that?" He talks about her with such disdain.

"She was my friend, my only friend." I must get out of this

suffocating place, but Philip holds my arm, puts his hands around me, not letting me leave. His lips whisper soothing words to me, but all I want is to curl up in a teeny-tiny ball and hide at the same time.

"I'm so sorry, but we are at war; the Germans want to kill us all."

"She died because of me, if not for me she wouldn't be dead now, how will I go on?" My hands try to push him away, but he holds me firmly against his body.

"She did not die because of you; she died because of the Germans. You must listen to me; she did not die because of you." He whispers to me again and again, his lips close to mine.

But I know he's lying. He's lying to me that she didn't die because of me, and he's lying to me that they wouldn't throw me to the German dogs if I'm not efficient enough. Or maybe they will ask their Communist friends to do the dirty work for them, when it's time to kill me, and he's lying to me with his hands hugging my body.

"I'm not angry at you. I'll be the best soldier you've got, I promise."

"I'm so sorry, but you must never forget who you are."

"I'm a French warrior." And my hands push his hug away as I turn from the wall and run up the stairs. I must get out of this dim basement. For a moment, I stop in the alley and wipe away my tears, noticing that I haven't said goodbye to him, but I can't go back into that dark place. Anyway, it doesn't matter at all; he doesn't care about me. To them, I'm just a replaceable girl in an occupied city.

I head to Lizette's house as fast as I can, quietly climbing the stairs into the attic where I live, closing the door behind me without turning on the light. Let the black night surround me.

***

I wonder what it's like to fly and hit the sidewalk. The first rays of the sun paint the grey roof panels in yellow, while my feet slowly approach the edge of the building, and I'm carefully looking down at the street, examining the hard-paved stones.

For almost a year, I have been living here on the sixth floor, and in all that time, my attic window stayed closed. Even the spectacular view of the city rooftops, and the Eiffel Tower in the distance, did not convince me to open the window and step carefully onto the grey zinc boards.

It's too frightening for me, sitting on the edge and looking at the city, in what could be considered a nest of privacy for a reclusive girl or an escape route when needed. But not for me, I'm too scared of the height and the street below.

What is it like to fly in the air? How did she feel? Did she know it was the end? Was landing on the pavement painful to her? I straighten up to stand on the grey roof panel, feeling it shake under my body weight, while I spread my arms to the sides and lift my chin, breathing the cool morning breeze and closing my eyes. Just one more small step.

I can't feel so guilty anymore, I'm just one girl who wanted to live, and I can't turn the clock back.

Why did I manage to escape from the police a year ago? Where are Dad and Mom and Jacob? Why did the railway worker knock me down that day, stopping me from running to the barbed wire fences?

"There's no one there anymore. They took everyone," he'd shouted at me and pushed me onto the railway, making me scream in pain. Why didn't I return to that place and try again?

My eyes look at the street below,

the man walking on his way to work, looking like a small drop of paint on the grey street, the Eiffel Tower in the distance painted a reddish hue in the first rays of the sun. I can even see the Nazi flag shining in the morning rays.

"I must live." My legs bend as if on their own, and I sit on the edge, holding the metal plates tightly, and writing Mathilde's words with my fingers on the morning dew which covers the grey roof panel.

The morning rays will soon erase the words, and the street downstairs is waiting for me; it's time to decide. What should I do?

What would Mom do?

Carefully I close the small window to the roof, making sure to lock the latch as hard as I can. Claudine did not die because of me; she died because of the Germans.

***

"You're late," Simone tells me as I close the glass door behind me, gasping from the fast walk, but she hands me the clean apron from the hanger and even smiles at me as I wear it, taking my position behind the counter. Soon the first customer will walk through the door. I am a French warrior, and I am willing to do whatever it takes to live.

***

The German Officer

June, 1943

Secret 6/18/1943

From: Western Front Wehrmacht Command

To: Army Group France

Subject: Preparations for opening a new western front

Background: Due to the Allied invasion of Sicily, we estimate that the Italian army will surrender to the enemy.

General: By the orders of the Führer Hitler, offensive operations on the eastern front in Russia will cease immediately. We estimate that in the coming year, a naval landing will be executed from the direction of England through the La Manche canal.

Tasks:

Construction of a protective barrier along the western beaches.

Construction of protective bunkers to protect the Führer's secret weapon of revenge against London.

Method: Army Group France will be reinforced with engineering divisions that will be mobilized from the Eastern Front and the South Italy Front.

The headquarters of the engineering division for the canal section will be located in Paris.

Finding houses for the division's headquarters officers will be the responsibility of maintenance battalion 411.

SS. Telegram 445

Violette and Anaïs

Once in a few days, I see them. Usually, I notice them through the boulangerie window. They tend to stand patiently outside the shop, waiting for their spouses to finish buying the morning patisseries for them. Their dresses are glamorous, in the best fashion the summer of 1943 allows women, especially those who tend to enjoy German money. I watch their wavy hairstyles with envy, and they remind me of the famous movie star known for her warm attitude towards high-ranking German officers. With a hug, they greet their spouses as they walk out of the store, biting off the crispy croissants that were baked in robbed French butter.

"Monique, stop staring at the street outside, have you served the gentleman in the black uniform?"

"Yeah, he's waiting for the fresh pastry tray that will be out in a minute."

Their spouses are wearing neatly-ironed grey-green officers' uniforms, and with their cropped blonde hair and perfect smile, they could appear on any German Army recruitment poster.

"Danke." They thank me as I put the fresh pastries in the paper bag, and my eyes follow them as they rush to serve the fine butter to the girls my age who are waiting for them outside the boulangerie.

"They have money," says Simone after they disappear down the street.

"They have German army officers,"
I answer, and Simone smiles a bit.

'Arletty & Arletty' always wait
outside for their gentlemen to
arrive, but today the pouring rain
has driven them in, and they
gently close the door behind them.
As I examine them, they shake
their wavy hair from the raindrops
and approach me, the short one
with a shy smile and the tall one
with a defiant look.

"Good morning, we did not want to
wait for them in the rain," the tall
one with the lush brown hair tells
me, and I notice that she has a
small gap between her front teeth.

"Good morning, is it okay if we
order? Can we?" the short one
joins in; she's my height and has
a delicate face and big eyes, the

kind I always dreamed I would
have when I still dared to dream of
being a movie star.

"Good morning, what would you
like?"

"Can I have a baguette?" the tall
one asks; she has thick, beautiful
lips.

"Can I have a baguette too?" the
little one asks with an embarrassed
smile, and I watch her delicate lips.

"Anaïs." The brown-haired woman
reaches her hand beyond the
counter.

"Violette." The other joins and
reaches her hand too.

"Nice to meet you, Monique." I
give them my hand, and for the
first time I touch hands that have
caressed a German soldier.

What would Mom think of me if she knew? Why couldn't I have found them a year ago, even though I tried?

✳✳✳

"Luckily, the Germans are cleaning the streets of them; there is no food left in France, because of their greediness." I heard those two women in a grocery store, about a year ago. They were complaining about the butter ration, and my eyes remained lowered to the floor, carefully examining my old shoes.

"It's time for the Germans to put things in order on this issue," the other one agreed with her. "My sister told me there were even policemen who warned them to run and hide before the raid." Why did no policeman come to warn Dad?

For a moment, I looked at them, but I lowered my eyes again; no one else intervened in their conversation, and a few other women standing in line nodded their approval.

"At least they crammed all of them in camp Drancy; from there, they will no longer be able to rule the world." Another woman joined the conversation.

"Are you giving up your turn?" The older one between them asked me.

"Yes, I forgot my ration stamps at home." I answered her, and ran out of the grocery store.

* * *

My feet carried me towards the massive building and the barbed wire fences surrounding it. As I kept getting closer, passing the metal sign 'Drancy', I started to get scared. "They are waiting for me," I tried to encourage myself, to keep walking on the rails leading to the camp, but a railway worker wearing dirty clothes stood in my way.

"Hey, you, where are you going?"

"I have to find something."

"This is not a place for a girl like you, get out of here."

"I need to know something."

"It will cost you." He looked at me lustfully.

"I can give you that," I handed him

my monthly butter ration stamps, my hand shaking, not knowing how I would explain the loss of our butter ration to Lizette.

"What do you want to know?" His black fingers collected the stamps, quickly shoving them into his pocket.

"My family, I need to meet them. I have to; please help me." My gaze focused on the grey building and the little figures walking between the barbed wire fences. I had to meet them.

"Are you Jewish?"

"No."

"They were taken east by train, to Auschwitz camp."

"Please, I must find them." My

fingers quickly dug into the bag, handing him our meat ration stamps. "That's all I have."

"You cannot find them; they are in Poland now, go away from here, it is dangerous for you, they will take you too." He turned and walked away from me, refusing to take the meat stamps from my hand.

"What are you doing?" the train worker shouted at me as I started running towards the fences.

"I have to say goodbye to them," I shouted as I gasped and stepped up, not thinking whether he heard or understood my words.

"They will catch you and send you there too." He dropped me on the rails, made me scream from the pain of the fall.

"I did not have time to say goodbye to them," I whimpered into his shoulder as it pressed me to the ground, feeling the rails hurt my body and smelling the diesel and grease from his dirty clothes. "I have to, I have to say goodbye to them." I cried and tried to fight him off, wanting to keep running toward the fences and the people behind them.

"You must not; there is no point, they are no longer there, it is not them, they have been taken, now they hold POWs and American pilots whose planes have been shot down." He kept pinning me to the ground, not releasing me until he was sure I'd calmed down and stopped crying, and would not keep running.

"I'm sorry, they're not there

anymore." I felt his grip loosen as he stood up, stabilizing himself and looking at me for a moment, moving away from me but staying close in case I got up and started running towards the fences again. When I finally got up off the rails and looked at him walking away, I noticed my butter ration stamps thrown on the rails beside my old shoes.

"What do you think of my new shoes?" Violette asks me a few days after we first met, as she blushes and raises her leg so I can see them.

"They are very beautiful." I bend over the counter; they are gorgeous.

"I told you she's nice." Violette laughs at Anaïs.

"She received them as a special gift," Anaïs adds a piece of information as she leans back against the wall, and Violette blushes even more, smiling awkwardly.

"Come walk with us down the avenue after work, please, the weather is nice," she asks.

"I do not know; I need to get home."

"The days are much warmer now; please join us." She looks at me with her big, round, dark eyes, as if begging for my company.

"Yes, that would be nice," Anaïs adds from the side as she sizes me up, and the apron I am wearing.

And I let them convince me, promising myself I'll be distant when we walk together, but meanwhile I say goodbye to them until the end of the day. I have no choice but to meet them; Philip expects me to bring him more information.

I arrange the croissants left on the trays in straight lines, placing the baguettes in the basket in order; what kind of smiles shall I show them? Cleaning the tables until they are shiny, checking and making sure there is no dirt on my dress, and washing the shop window facing the street, thinking what I will say. Slowly I return the change to the customer in the grey-green uniform, trying to avoid looking at the clock hanging above the door. Too soon, the end of the day arrives. They are not my friends; they'll never be, my stomach hurts.

"We need to hurry. They are already waiting for us." Violette rushes me as we walk to the metro, and I think I have not walked the boulevard since what happened to Claudine.

"Who is waiting for us?" I stop walking, surprised.

"Our guys." Anaïs smiles at me as if to confess a secret. "They've wanted to meet you for a long time."

"You did not tell me they were coming too."

"We told you, but you were too busy arranging all your baguettes and didn't listen to us." Violette laughs at me. "Don't be afraid;

they don't bite, after you know them, you'll change your mind about German soldiers."

"They can teach you a lot of new things, ask Violette," Anaïs adds while Violette looks down, blushing.

"We must hurry, you can't change your mind now, I promised them you were coming." Violette takes my hand, and I walk with them, knowing they had not told me before. They must have been afraid I would refuse to join them, but now it's too late.

"I can stand it," I whisper to myself as we reach the stairs leading down to the Metro Opera station, passing a man in a long coat, his eyes staring at me.

"She's with us." Anaïs glares at him indifferently as she grabs my hand and pulls me after her down the stairs.

I'll never be one of them; I think to myself as we ride in the cramped metro car, I'll never go out with a German soldier.

***

"Monique, meet Fritz and Fritz." And for the first time in my life, I'm shaking hands with a German soldier, and I want to scream.

They smile at me very politely when I lower my eyes from their blue ones, introducing themselves formally. Their names are not Fritz and Fritz, but in all the storm blowing through my head, I cannot hear anything else as I try to smile back and raise my head. They reach their hands out to me, and I touch them for a split-second and pull my hand back quickly, feeling my palm burning. If only I had thought to bring gloves with me.

"We already know you," they say together. "From the boulangerie. You're the nice saleswoman."

"There was another girl, but we don't see her anymore, she was nice too, what happened to her?"

"She doesn't work there anymore." I rub my palm, pressing it firmly with my fingers.

"What about us?" Violette asks, and gets a warm hug from her fair-haired Fritz.

"We are here just for decoration," says Anaïs while she places her arm on the back of her private Fritz, bringing him closer to a long kiss while turning her back to me. "Shall we go?"

Had they notice that I held back when they touched my hand? I must learn to control myself, to make Philip proud of me. Their attention is on their girls as we walk down the avenue. They are watching all the people enjoying the summer afternoon, and my eyes are focused on Violette's fingers playing with Fritz's grey-green jacket.

The cafés are full of German soldiers and their accompanying young girls; the group is trying to locate a place to sit while I walk a little behind them; maybe the passersby will think I'm just looking in the shop windows and I'm not one of them.

"What do you think?" Everyone stops and looks at me.

"Sorry, I didn't hear you."

"What do you think of the new movie that came out?"

"What movie?"

"The movie we were talking about, with the French actress Arletty."

"I haven't seen it yet."

"Will you join us to see it? They say she plays wonderfully." Violette looks at me questioningly.

"I don't know; my evenings are usually busy."

What do the people on the street think of me? Do they spit or curse at us when they pass on the sidewalk? I feel as if strangers' eyes are staring at my back, penetrating me with hateful looks. I must learn to fit in with them.

 "I would be happy to go if I had a day off."

"Great, you'll enjoy spending time with us." Anaïs looks at me and smiles. What does she think of me?

"Maybe next time we'll take care of Monique? So you won't have to hang out with us so lonely?" she adds as she turns to her Fritz and hugs him, making me look down.

"It's okay; I'm having a good time on my own."

"It's a great idea." Violette holds my arm with enthusiasm. "It's a lot more fun to walk down the avenue together."

After I say goodbye to them and start walking home, I hurry away from the Champs Élysées and the noisy cafés. But even on the quiet street, I can imagine the stares at my back, as if they remained and hurt my skin. Even my palm is still hot, burning from the touch of their hands.

"Are you okay, my dear? How was your day?" Lizette asks me when I enter her warm living room, and I shake my head and say nothing. I cannot tell her who I hang out with and why. What would Lizette think of me if she knew? Would she stab my back with her glare too? Or throw me out of the attic she'd given me as a place to sleep?

At night, before bed, I try to comfort myself; the first time is always the hardest, like when I was a girl and Dad took me to the Tuileries Gardens playground.

"Roll over, it's okay, the first time is always the scariest," he assured me in his calm voice, as I sat crying at the end of the ladder, afraid to go down. "After the first time, you will get used to and enjoy the feeling."

'Are you also getting used to Auschwitz camp?' I ask him in my imagination, but he does not answer me.

***

I haven't met him since that time he hurt me so much, after Claudine was killed, and I go downstairs in fear. How should I behave in front of him? How will he react?

He is waiting for me as always, at the bottom of the stairs, and we approach each other slowly, step by step.

"You are quiet." He is standing close to me.

"I have nothing to say."

"Say something,"

"I'm trying to learn and get better." Even though I haven't forgiven him, I stay close to him.

"How are you?" Philip doesn't walk away either.

"Working at the boulangerie as usual."

"And how is your new place? Is it comfortable?" He does not mention the name of the one I killed.

"I feel great." Nor do I.

"Does Simone treat you nicely?"

"Yes, she treats me well, and I've already met two new girlfriends."

"That's good." Philip leans back, that's probably what he thinks of me, that I hurried to replace dead Claudine with the living Anaïs and Violette.

"And how are they, those two new girlfriends of yours?"

"They are very nice, they usually hang out with German soldiers, so I am joining them." I also lean back, thinking of Claudine and her Messerschmitt pilot, the one who courted her for days, but disappeared when she lay in a simple wooden coffin.

"And is it good for you? To go out with them?"

"What's good for France is good for me."

"I'm happy." He walks away from me, and I can no longer smell his body odor.

"They want to bring someone else with them, their officer. They suggested I go out with him."

"And will you do it?" He turns his back to me; doesn't want to look at me at all.

"Yes, I'm willing to do it." After I killed Claudine, it's my turn to take her place. At least, that's what he expects me to do; the only reason he's kept me alive.

"Thanks." I hear his voice, though

he is standing with his back to me. He will not stop me from hanging out with a German officer; he will keep his distance from me, waiting for my reports, sending me back to him, without asking me how scared I am. He won't hug me like last time; I do not want him to hug me anymore.

"I have a lot of new information to report."

"So sit down and report." Philip slowly turns to me and leads me to the small wooden table, touching my arm for a moment.

"What new information do you have?"

Now that Claudine is dead, I have a lot to tell him. All day I listen and remember, concentrating on all those soldiers who think I'm a stupid Frenchwoman who does not understand the German language, opening their big mouths and gossiping to their friends while waiting to see my smile.

"The Germans are starting to fortify the beaches against possible invasion. They have moved new engineering divisions from the East, and I will be much more efficient after I go out with my new friends and their acquaintances." But Philip does not place his fingers on mine, even though they are waiting on the table. I don't want him to touch me.

"Do not forget that they are not your friends."

"No one is my friend." I pull my hands away from the simple wooden board and say goodbye to him. He could have been nicer to me after he made sure I would be left without a friend.

* * *

"He's really nice," Violette whispers to me excitedly a few days later, when they enter the boulangerie.

"And he's high-ranking, they call his rank 'Oberst' in German, he has a lot of privileges as an officer. A lot of privileges are good for Monique," adds Anaïs with a secret smile, while taking a bite from the croissant I gave her.

"And he's lonely here in Paris." Violette continues, not understanding I have been waiting for their trap, knowing I would have to step inside and fall.

For days I've been hoping that maybe their German officer would change his mind, or be moved with his unit from Paris. Whenever the glass door opened and the bell rung, I looked up apprehensively and let out a sigh of relief when the entrants were German soldiers, not Violette and Anaïs. But now both of them stand in front of me, waiting for my acceptance.

"I'm not sure I'll be an interesting companion to him."

"You are beautiful, believe me, he will be interested in you," Anaïs looks at me and takes a box of cigarettes out of the fashionable handbag, but after she notices Simone's look, she chooses to return the package inside her bag.

"Will you come with us on Saturday?" Violette smiles at me.

"Monique, there are customers."

I want to ask Anaïs what she means, that he will be interested in me, but Simone calls me again.

"What's his name?" I have to go back to work.

"His name is Ernest, Oberst Ernest."

✱✱✱

Oberst Ernest

"You should put lipstick on." Lizette hands me the red tube as I stand in front of the mirror, getting ready for the meeting.

My fingers tremble as I slide the soft burgundy tip over my lips, feeling its softness and weird taste for the first time.

"Let me help you." Lizette takes the lipstick from my hand and gently holds my chin while I concentrate on her brown eyes.

"There you go, look in the mirror." She smiles at me with satisfaction, and I stare at the woman I become, trying to get used to my new me.

"Where are you going?" she'd

asked me earlier when I was on my way to the door, hurrying to get outside and trying to avoid her.

"I've met someone." I immediately regretted telling her, afraid she would ask more.

"You can't go out like that."

"This is my nicest dress." I looked embarrassed in my simple beige dress, not knowing what to answer her, but she took me by my hand to her bedroom, ignoring me telling her that I was already late.

I was detained all morning, opening and closing the attic window, looking at the grey zinc tiles and the street below.

"You're a woman; you need to be at your best." She sits me in the chair in front of the dresser and starts combing my hair, turning it into the smooth waves of a movie star.

"What do you think?" she asks after helping with the lipstick.

"It's lovely; thank you."

I'd always dreamed of looking like that, but Mom never agreed to it. The only time she ever slapped me was when she caught me putting on pink lipstick I'd bought with a shaking hand, in those days before the warrants. We were still allowed to go into cosmetics stores, at least the ones far from the German headquarters. "Only prostitutes wear makeup like that!" she shouted, and tossed the lipstick in the trash as I ran from her, locking myself in my room and stroking my aching cheeks, hating her, and wishing she would be gone.

"Are you excited about the date?"

"A little bit, but I'm okay." I dab the tip of my eye. Where is she now?

"Something's missing," Lizette pulls a light pink scarf from the brown closet in her bedroom and ties it around my neck, looking at me with a satisfied look and hugging me warmly. "Take care of yourself."

"Thank you; I won't be late." My legs carry me down the stairs, wanting to get away from Lizette's warm hugs and all the lies I'm telling her. Maybe it's better Mom can't see me like this, not knowing who I'm going to meet.

I have to hurry; they are probably waiting for me.

Even though I've never met him before, I can recognize him from a distance and slow down, stopping and breathing deeply. They are all standing and chatting near the café where we'd arranged to meet. Fritz and Fritz stand tall, not moving, next to them are Violette and Anaïs dressed in cheerful cream-colored dresses, and they all give him respect.

He stands alone in a relaxed position and is a little taller than Phillip; he has short light hair rather than a dark quiff, and his uniforms are clean grey-green, decorated with many medals and ranks, not dirty with black printing stains. But as I stand at a distance, looking at him, I notice that he also has a pistol stuck in his belt. However, his firearm is hidden in a shiny new leather case.

Breathe slowly; I need to get close

to them; he is waiting for me.

"Ernest, nice to meet you." He notices me, extends his hand, and I force myself to take the small steps left between us.

"Monique, nice to meet you." He looks at me with his green eyes, and I'm shiver

"Shall we sit down?"

And as we step between the tables outside, waiting for the waiter to accompany us to our reserved table, I feel his hand gently touch my waist, taking ownership of me. At any time, I can change my mind and back off.

"I understand you work in a boulangerie shop," he asks me politely as we sit down, after holding the chair for me; no one has ever done that before.

"Yes."

"And what do you do there?"

"I'm just selling croissants and baguettes."

"You should try them, their croissants are amazing." Violette joins the conversation.

"Maybe I'll do that one day," he smiles at her, returning his attention to me. "Do you like your job?"

"Very much," I try to be cordial as I can. "What do you do in the army?"

"Engineering matters, not something that would interest young women like you. We shouldn't talk about the army; we should talk about art and the superb culinary heritage that brings such splendid food to our mouths." I look down and feel the taste of the lipstick on my lips.

"Danke." He thanks the waiter who places the wine glasses on the table, not noticing the slight reluctance in the waiter's face. From a nearby table, I can smell real coffee. I missed that smell so much. How do I start a conversation with a German officer who frightens me?

"What do you like in our splendid Paris?"

"Well, Paris is still new to me; we were stationed here not long ago; it will take me some time to learn everything the city has to offer. Zum wohl, ladies." He raises his glass of wine in the air, and as commanded, everyone reaches out and holds their drinks. "To our lovely hostess in our splendid Paris, may we stay here forever."

"Zum wohl." Everyone smiles and clinks glasses, sipping the wine, and I choke. I must get used to the taste.

"Are you okay?" He turns his attention to me.

"Yes, I'm okay, I'm not used to red wine."

"Shall I order you a different wine?" He raised his hand in command, calling the waiter.

"No, no, that's okay." But he is already giving instructions to the waiter, and within a moment a cold bottle of champagne appears on the table, with new glasses.

"And again, cheers," Ernest raises his glass, "to a new German-French friendship." I take a small sip of the sweet liquid, avoiding telling him I'm not used to drinking at all.

We only had some wine on Friday evenings. Dad would pass the Kiddush glass of wine carefully from one to another, letting us taste the sweet red flavor, but that too had gone two and a half years ago, in that terrible winter, when we almost ran out of food.

"The food here is delicious, so delicate, many flavors, for that I must admit, French cuisine surpasses German." And everyone agrees.

"At least they know how to do one thing properly, unlike fighting." says Violette's Fritz, and everyone laughs, except Oberst Ernest, who looks at me.

"And what about the beautiful women they manage to bring into our hands?" Fritz of Anaïs donates his part, and everyone rejoices, laughing when she kisses him on the lips. Oberst Ernest continues to smile at me, his polite smile; I don't want him to.

"It is so nice here on the boulevard." Violette contributes to the conversation.

"To a lasting partnership for a thousand years." Anaïs raises the glass of wine, and everyone joins.

Later, after eating a pie with real cherry, flour and sugar, we march on the Champs Élysées, and even though I try, I can no longer separate myself. What do passersby think of me?

"Do you enjoy our company?" Ernest asks me, navigating the two of us so we can walk a few steps ahead of the rest.

"Yeah, everything's fine. I'm just not used to going out like that."

"How come?"

"I'm not like Violette and Anaïs; I'm less Parisian than they are."

"Where is the place you call home?"

"I grew up in Strasbourg and also in Dunkirk." I'm thinking of my real home, the one I left running. Is he waiting for me? I never went back, too afraid to be recognized; what if someone calls my name again while I'm walking beside a German officer?

"Monique?"

"Sorry, I was thinking about my childhood home."

"In Strasbourg?"

"Yes, I apologize for not listening."

"If you grew up in Strasbourg, do you speak German?" He moves to his language.

"Like a native," I answer him in German.

"And all this time, you let me struggle with my French?"

Had I annoyed him? I stop walking and look into his green eyes, trying to read the expression on his face, but I can't. What should I answer?

"We're in Paris, I was taught that a man should strive for a woman." And he laughs out loud.

"You have courage. I love that in a woman." And I think that if he knew me, he would have known how cowardly I am, but I keep on looking in his eyes and say nothing for a moment before lowering my eyes, not wanting to cross the line.

"And when did you move to Paris?" he continues.

"It's hard for me to talk about it," I allow myself to answer him. "And when did you get to Paris?"

"A month ago."

"And where had you been before?"

"It's hard for me to talk about it." He smiles at me as if we have found a shared secret that brings us closer, and I try to smile back, wondering if I have any more lipstick left on my lips. Maybe I should have gone to the restrooms earlier and get organized? Like Anaïs?

"What are you talking about?" Violette interjects between us, as per an agreed-upon sign which ended the allotted time of a young couple's privacy on their first date.

"Museums and art," Ernest answers her as he watches me.

"I do not like museums; they bore me," she answers him.

"And you?" He turns the question to me.

"I like them." I think that's what he wants to hear.

I never liked museums. Ever since I was a child, walking with the whole class, looking up in fear at the enormous threatening paintings of people fighting, injuring each other, cutting off their heads, while the teacher spoke passionately about the duty of sacrifice for the homeland. But three years ago, I really started hating them. It was on that class trip to the Louvre when we came to a sign at the entrance: "Jews are not allowed." And the teacher took Sylvie and I out of the line, sending us home, while everyone grinned or looked at us sadly. I hated their pitying looks.

"Would you like to go with me to the Louvre? I always wanted to see the huge paintings of Napoleon with my own eyes, to watch all his battles and victories."

"I would be happy to join you if it interests you."

"Like you, I'm the quiet type and find it difficult to connect with the Parisian bustle. I prefer to watch the art of the great painters." And I manage to smile at him again as if we have found another thing that connects us, the desire for silence.

***

The street is quiet in the evening, and even though I enjoy the silence, I rise from the bench in the garden and start walking to the place I call home. It is already late, and the small attic is waiting for me.

After we said goodbye, I could not return to Lizette; I had to relax for a few minutes. We all stood under the Arc de Triomphe, looking at the figures engraved in marble, while Fritz and Fritz talked about Napoleon's victories, and Ernest gently held my waist, leading me apart from the others.

"Monique, I've enjoyed getting to know you. You were a perfect companion."

"Danke," I answer him in German.

"I would be happy to invite you to see me again."

"I'd like that too." I know this is the only answer he expects to hear.

He bowed formally and came a little closer, kissing my hand, and I can smell his body scent mixed with quality male perfume.

"Good night, Mademoiselle Monique, we'll meet again in a

quiet place." He smiles at me, talking in French.

"Good night, Herr Oberst Ernest," I answer him in German and slowly start walking away, turning my back to him.

"How is he?" Violette catches me before I walk away. "He's very nice, isn't he?"

"So what do you think of him?" Anaïs joins her, arriving in a peaceful walk. "You'd better get him for yourself."

"How did it feel to me?" I ask myself later, as I sit alone on the bench in the street, rubbing my palm where his lips kissed it and holding my aching belly.

"How is he?" Lizette asks me when I enter her apartment.

"He's nice and polite."

"Will you join me for coffee?" And even though I'm afraid of her questions, I accompany her to the kitchen.

"He was very polite, and he was clean," I try to describe Oberst Ernest to her.

"It is important."

"It's not easy to make a decision."

"It usually isn't."

"How did you get to know your husband?" I dare to ask as we relax on the couch, sipping the bitter and disgusting sugarless coffee of war.

"I wasn't polite, but it was a long time ago," she smiles at me.
"We met at a demonstration for

women's suffrage, before the previous war."

"Please tell me."

"I was a rebellious girl from a rich family, and he was a young bank clerk who volunteered to help us carry our protest signs when we escaped from the police."

"And what happened next?" I'm happy to divert the conversation away from me.

"He was killed, and we still don't have voting rights like men do, so it probably wasn't that successful."

"That's sad."

"Yes, life is sad sometimes, but the look in his eyes was worth it all." She smiles for a moment, and I lower my eyes from his picture above the fireplace, concentrating on the bitter black cup between my hand.

Later, before going to bed, I stand in front of the mirror in my attic, scrutinizing myself.

The face has remained the same; the lipstick is long gone, the hair has also returned to its original shape, the waist and breasts remain the same, nothing has changed.

Dad was right; the second time is much easier, even the stabs in my back from the looks of passersby are almost unnoticed.

"Good night to you, licking German boots, Frenchie," I whisper to myself before turning off the light. What shall I say to Philip next time I meet him?

***

The afternoon sunlight paints the city roofs in shades of gold, but the rays do not penetrate the dirty alley of the Latin Quarter, leaving the street grey as I walk to meet him.

What does it matter what I say to him? All that he cares about is the information I bring with me. He doesn't care about me. My legs almost trip over a broken wooden crate that was thrown into the street, and a woman in the opposite store examines me while her little daughter is holding her feet firmly, curiously peeking at me and my new dress.

The stairs to the basement are waiting for me; I have to learn how to stay alive, to give him what he expects from me.

Philip is waiting for me at the bottom of the stairs, in the same alert position; I mustn't get excited by him, he will not protect me if he has to choose.

"I've been waiting too long for you." He tries to get closer, but I pass him and go inside, smelling him for a split-second.

"I arrived as quickly as I could," I answer, keeping my distance from him.

"Did you meet him?"

"I met him."

Philip says nothing, just walking around the small basement, examining me with his dark eyes.

"We all went out together, walking down the avenue, and we also sat in a café. He ordered me champagne."

For a moment, he approaches, still silent, as if to grab me by force and shake my body, but he stops himself. Why don't you say something?

"And we talked a lot about museums and art. He would like to take me on a visit to the Louvre. I can't wait to walk to the Louvre."

Can anything hurt you? Like you hurt me?

"And he asked to meet me again, and I accepted his invitation, isn't that what you wanted in the first place? That I get more German information?"

"What German information did you get?" he asks in a distant voice.

"They are starting to mobilize forces for the fortifications of the coasts, and they call the project 'The Atlantic Wall,' they assume the invasion will take place in the coming year through Pas-de-Calais. They employ forced laborers to build the fortifications, and he admires Napoleon, especially his journey to Moscow." I pause for a moment to breathe, but Philip still says nothing, just listening to me as he grips the back of the old wooden chair.

"And your officer told you all that information?"

"His name is Ernest, and his rank is Oberst."

"And your Oberst Ernest told you all that information?"

"No, I understood all this from conversations between them, when they thought we women were only interested in wine and cherry pies. But Oberst Ernest also talked to me about art."

"Yes, I understood you like to talk about art."

"Do you like art?" Why does he never tell me anything about himself?

"And is there any more information you received from your Oberst Ernest?"

"Why do I know nothing about you? What did you do before the war?"

"What does it matter what I did before the war? The war is the general who decides what we have to do and who we are; we are only the pawns." He looks at me, still distant.

"Oberst Ernest likes art." Has he always worked in a printing house? Will he ever tell me anything about himself?

"And did you get more information from Oberst Ernest who likes art?" He is not interested in me.

"No, but if you want, I will meet him again."

"Do it."

He does not touch me as we part, and on the way to Lizette's apartment I see the Arc de Triomphe in the distance, and feel

a pinch of envy for a moment,
remembering the last time he
hugged me before he hurt me
so much. If only things could be
different. Why can't I be happy like
Anaïs or Violette?

Violette

"Where's Anaïs?" I ask a few
days later when she enters the
boulangerie before I go home,
gently closing the door behind her.

"Today I've arrived alone." She
smiles at me.

"Would you like to have something
sweet?"

"Is there anything left?" Since becoming my friends, they stop by from time to time without their Fritzes, asking if I have anything for them at closing time. Some baguettes, perhaps sweet chocolate or butter croissants. With grateful fingers, they pick up the leftovers of the German soldiers at the end of the day.

"Yes, there are some pastries left. I'll pack them for you."

"I'll wait for you outside, is that okay?" she whispers to me when she notices Simone's look.

"It's fine. I'll join you in a moment." I gather the leftovers into a paper bag, wondering where Anaïs is.

"Young women need to have values," Simone quietly says while she counts the money in the cash register, looking at me as I'm rushing out.

"Is it okay for me to wait for you outside until you finish work?" she asks when I hand her the paper bag with the pastries, turning to go inside. I have to clean and close the place up.

"Is everything okay? Did something happen?"

"Everything's fine. I just wanted to walk with you a little bit. Can you?"

"Where is Anaïs?"

"Anaïs is with her Fritz, showing him Paris the way she knows how."

"Wait a minute," I go inside, hurry to clean the tables, and wonder what she wants to talk to me about.

"I would not choose such company," Simone keeps talking to herself, making sure I hear, but I ignore her; I have no other girlfriends to choose from; the last one died because of me.

"I'd be happy if we could be friends," she tells me as we walk in silence, passing the Lafayette Gallery store, which showcases the summer fashion for German officers' spouses.

"What do you mean?" I pretend I don't understand.

"The two of us never meet alone, walking together, telling each other our thoughts."

"I thought you and Anaïs were friends like that. I always see you together."

"Yeah, but Anaïs only does what is good for Anaïs, especially in relation to the entertainment side of life."

"I thought you liked spending time with her." I hold her arm. It seems like she needs it, but after a few steps, the contact between us feels fake to me, and I release my hand, continuing to walk beside her in silence.

"What do you think of these?" She stops by a lingerie store window, pointing to a white bra and garter belt.

"For whom?" I ask hesitantly; this is an expensive store for rich women. I have never worn such underwear; even Mom never dressed like that, telling me more than once that only prostitutes walk with garters.

"It's for me. Fritz wants us to do it." She finally speaks the frightening words, as if she has been preparing for this moment for a long time.

"Is he insisting on it?"

I have no experience with such things. Everything I know I learned from Claudine's stories, I have not even kissed anyone on the mouth, only read about it in the magazine, the one Mom ripped after she found it.

"Yeah, he says that if we're a couple, we should do it."

"And what does Anaïs say about that?"

"She does not know."

"And it does not bother you that

he..." And it is difficult for me to say the words.

"He says he loves me and that they are winning the war."

What shall I tell her? Shall I tell her all the jokes I hear in the boulangerie, listening to the German soldiers that don't know I speak their language? Shall I tell her about the Panzer tank man in the black uniform who laughed a few days ago?

"Shut up; I have an announcement," he'd raised his voice, and all the other soldiers got quiet. "Himmler announced that anyone who did not return from Russia in a coffin is entitled to receive a Sexual Disease Medal from a French prostitute." Shall I tell her how they all laughed about it?

And what about the soldier who added to the cheers of laughter: "We can receive it for free, the French girls ask for it." How much shall I tell her?

"Are you sure he loves you?"

"He told me that after the war is over and they win, he will marry me."

"And do you believe him?"

"I don't want to be hungry. Two years ago, in the winter, I was standing in line at the grocery store, shivering and holding the food ration tickets. I'd prayed for a sturdy man to come save me, and he came. So he is not French, but he is nice to me; I want to be on the winning side, not the hungry side." She doesn't stop talking, spilling her guts while we look out at the shop window, at a satin corset with a price tag that ensures the store has a stock of real tights.

"Wouldn't you act like me?" She looks at me.

What can I tell her? That in the winter, two years ago, we almost starved? I was standing last in the endless lines, only to find at the end of the day that there was no food left for the Jews? If Dad had not kept a few pounds of flour and oil hidden in the kitchen, I wouldn't be standing here beside her. Or maybe I can tell her that I know how to hide? Or that I'm learning about myself that I know how to lie much better than I thought I could?

"He's nice, but I'm afraid he just wants to get into your panties." I choose especially rude words, surprised at myself that I can say them.

But Violette laughs at my rude words, and she gives me her hand, and we keep walking down the boulevard like a couple of friends; why is she not Claudine? And why did no one tell me what a man does when he gets in your panties, and how does it feel?

***

"We have to tell you something."

Violette and Anaïs enter the boulangerie the next day while folding their arms and approaching the counter.

"We have an invitation to a picnic this weekend." Violette is excited.

"How are you today?" I try to whisper to her.

"Come with us? Please come." There is a pleading look in her eyes.

"Please come," Anaïs adds, "It's less interesting without the new girl."

"Sit down; I'll give you something." I have to serve a German soldier waiting in line. I want to ask Violette how she is, but she makes sure to stick to Anaïs.

"Here you go, two croissants, how are you?" I place the metal tray in front of them on the table in the corner. "Everything okay?" I whisper to her again, but she ignores my question.

"Yes, everything's okay." Anaïs

bends down and pulls a box of cigarettes out of her leather bag, puts a white cigarette in her mouth, and waits for one of the German soldiers to approach her with a lit lighter.

"Danke." She thankfully smiles at him while he proudly returns to his place in line. As she leans back and blows the bluish smoke toward the ceiling, her gaze wanders between Violette and me, as if trying to find a hidden connection.

"You should come," Anaïs looks at me. "Ernest will come too."

"Does he wants to meet me?"

"He said he would be happy if you could join us; he is not used to hearing the word 'no'."

I walk back to my place behind the counter, serving the other soldiers. I can do it, I can be nice to everyone, give them what they want, Violette, Oberst Ernest, Philip, even Simone.

"Monique, the customer is waiting," I hear Simone's impatient voice. Probably after Violette and Anaïs leave, she will mention that she does not like them and that only immoral, promiscuous women smoke, especially in public. I'm not like them.

"Monique, you have your chores to do."

"Sorry, I apologize." I have chores to do; Phillip also said I should do what is needed, even though he is not really interested in me. I smile and apologize to the soldier who is waiting, handing him the pastries and the change. Despite Simone's examining look, I approach Violette and Anaïs for a moment.

"Where is the picnic going to take place?"

"They are taking us to the Marne river, do you like water?"

I have never been to the Marne river.

***

Marne River, Northeast of Paris

"Come on, Monique, Anaïs, don't give up, we are beating them!" Violette's screams are heard over the quiet river, frightening some ducks, and they flee from the serenity of the riverbank, spreading their wings and passing over us in a peaceful flock.

"Come on, don't give up; they are getting tired." She continues to cheer us with loud shouts, and even though the three of us are panting heavily while holding the paddles, hitting the water in an attempt to maintain a steady pace, we have no chance against them. The officers' walnut-colored boat is far ahead of us, their paddles hitting the water uniformly as they listen to the sound of Oberst Ernest, giving them a rhythm in his quiet voice.

Earlier, with the first rays of sunshine, we three girls met at the foot of the Arc de Triomphe, waiting for them and examining each other. They had more beautiful dresses than mine, why didn't I put lipstick on my lips like them?

The two bored cops guarding the gate barely addressed us, but I walked away from them, making sure to be closer to Violette, even though since that time we talked she has told me nothing, avoiding me when I ask.

"Guten morgen," the officers greet us warmly as the open-roof army vehicle stops next to us with a squeak of the brakes, causing me to freeze for a moment, watching the cops near the Arc step back and look down.

"Guten morgen, how are we all going to get in here?" Violette asks and laughs.

"They'll tie one of us on the car hood like a hunted deer," Anaïs offers.

"If anything, then a rabbit or a fox," Ernest answers her and smiles at me. "Good morning, Mademoiselle Monique."

"Good morning, Herr Oberst Ernest."

"You girls will sit in the back with us," Fritz answers her. And they seat me respectfully next to Ernest,

who is in the driver's seat, while
everyone else huddles in the back,
Fritz next to Fritz and Violette
sitting on the knees of the giggling
Anaïs, close to Fritz's knees.

"I'm glad you chose to join us,"
Ernest quietly whispers as he
exchanges a hidden smile with me.

"I'm happy too," I answer him
quietly, returning a small smile
while my fingernails scratch my
palms, fearing he's noticed.

***

"And now, everyone pay attention,
we'll teach you a German song,"
Fritz announces from the back
seat, trying to overcome the
whistling wind on the ride and

Violette's laugh. And we all follow him, line by line, shouting the chorus as I translate the words into French for the two girls. Even Ernest allows himself to sing quietly while he concentrates on driving, his hands clad in black gloves gripping the steering wheel tightly, and occasionally he glances at me.

"Ihhhh... this is a dirty song," Violette announces in a protest of laughter as I translate the last line, hoping Ernest does not notice that it is difficult for me to say these words.

"That's how it is; we are rude people," Fritz informs us with a laugh and chooses a new song to study, while the morning sun lights our way.

Near a small town, we turn onto a dirt road and park the car on the riverbank near an empty dock, where two walnut-colored wooden rowboats are waiting for us, painted with shiny varnish.

"Just for us," Fritz announces while I wait for Ernest to come out and open the door for me, learning to be a woman.

"You thought of everything," Violette expresses admiringly.

"That's who we are, singing dirty songs and planning everything," Fritz lifts her in the air while she laughs and blushes.

"Shall we share equally?" Fritz suggests.

"I think it's time for France against Germany," Anaïs offers.

"The girls against the boys."
Violette joins her. I have a feeling
Ernest is interested in a different
division, but he says nothing and
gives me a little smile as I join
them, waiting for Fritz to stabilize
our boat, gripping it to the dock to
make it easier for us to get into it.

"France is winning," Violette
announces as we start rowing,
not waiting for the men to get
into their boat. Still, they easily
close the gap, leaving us far
behind despite Violette's shouts of
encouragement.

"We were defeated, we are yours,"
Violette dramatically announces as
we get out of the boat and climb
to the bank, spreading her arms
to the sides and lying down on the
green grass.

"Did you enjoy it?" Ernest asks as he serves me a meat sandwich, and I nod my head, wondering if they ever miss anything.

"Come and join us; it's not good to sit alone with a German officer." Anaïs takes me by my arm, leading us behind one of the trees while Ernest follows me with a smiling look.

"What are you doing?"

"Changing into a swimsuit."

"A swimsuit?"

"Yes, the river is nice and cool."

Shall I tell her I don't have a swimsuit at all? That my last swimsuit was from childhood, before my breasts had even grown? At home, no one thought

340

of sewing a yellow badge onto a bathing suit; we never thought of going for a swim in the river, too frightened by the German soldiers. In the warm summer, I used to walk through alternate streets, not wanting to see all the people sunbathing along the banks of the Seine.

"I did not bring a swimsuit with me. I did not think of it."

"Too bad," Violette looks at me sadly. "It can be enjoyable."

"You can jump in with your underwear. Ernest will love what he sees," giggles Anaïs as she arranges the straps of her blue swimsuit, checking that they are in place.

"Do you want me to give you my swimsuit?" Violette suggests,

"I don't mind going in with underwear." But I thank her and refuse, preferring to stay on the riverbank, I cannot expose myself like that to the eyes of men.

"Don't you want to swim in the river?" Ernest asks me as we emerge from behind the tree. They jump towards the dock and the water, and I turn to sit on the picnic blanket the men have spread out for us.

"I apologize. I forgot to bring my bathing suit."

"I've given up swimming. I do not want to get wet." He informs the Fritzes who have taken off their uniforms and placed them in an orderly manner as if in a parade, and he sits down next to me on the blanket. The Fritzes express only a minor protest before turning to throw the girls into the river and jumping into the cold water after them.

"Don't you like to swim?"

"I'm more a kind of land animal."

"I noticed that you also didn't put on lipstick, like the other girls."

What should I answer him?

"I wanted to be different from them. Do you like a woman to put lipstick on her lips?"

"I think a woman is more feminine if she behaves like an elegant woman." My lips feel naked all of a sudden.

"I'll try." I look down at the grass, feeling so simple compared to Anaïs' and Violette's dresses.

"What about poetry? After we talked last time, I was wondering whether you like poetry."

"Yes, I enjoy listening to poetry." When I was a young girl, before it all started, I would lie in bed, unable to sleep. The news reports at the cinema frightened me, showing Hitler's declarations of war and the vast endless army marching in rows towards the border.

They are just being threatening, Dad explained to me, the Germans are a cultured people, a nation that has brought poets and philosophers to the world like Heine, Ghetto, and Schiller will not kill just like that. With his hand caressing my hair, he suggested reading me their poems.

And I would sit in bed, patiently

waiting for him to return with a book in his hand. He would then sit next to me on the little chair, and start reading me poems. Dad, where are you now?

"Do you want me to read poetry to you?" He wakes me from my thoughts.

"I'd love that." And he gets up and goes to the car, returning after a moment holding a book and sitting next to me on the blanket.

"Shell I start to read?"

"Yes, please."

"Whoever has succeeded in the great attempt,

To be a friend's friend,

Whoever has won a lovely woman,

Add his to the jubilation!"

He reads Schiller's "Ode to Joy" to me in his quiet voice, and I close my eyes and hum the notes from memory as tears begin to flow from my eyes.

Tears for Dad's voice that I already have a hard time remembering, tears for not having time to say goodbye to him when the cops knocked on the door. Tears for the man that stopped my running at Drancey camp, and for what I became. Tears for not being hungry anymore, and for this hot, sunny day and the sounds of laughter coming from the river.

"I'm sorry if something I read hurt you, I apologize."

"No, it's okay. Thank you for reading to me."

He continues to read in his quiet

voice, and I find myself listening to him, but I am no longer able to contain the words, letting my thoughts fly to the east, looking at the water sparkling in the midday sun.

"You missed all the fun," Violette laughs as she comes running in all wet, looking for a towel and dripping on the blanket, causing Ernest to put the book away.

"What were you doing while we weren't watching?" Anaïs joins and lays herself on the spread blanket, panting and dripping as well.

"We read poetry." I smile at her as she grimaces.

"Do you know that great battles took place here in the previous war? That time, we lost to you, the French." Fritz joins us.

"I told them we would have beaten you if only we'd pushed harder," Violette answers while hugging his shoulders.

"Last time you won, and you managed to stop our attack on the riverbank, but not this time. This time no one will stop us." Ernest looks at Fritz appreciatively.

"You men are so boring with all your war talk," Violette gets up from the blanket and snatches Fritz's officer's hat, which lies on top of the pile of clothes, putting it on her head and standing in front of us with her hands on her hips.

"Achtung!" She straightens up and salutes, wearing the German officer's hat and a bathing suit, while everyone laughs. "Wait a minute," she gets excited by the theatrical moment and also picks up her Fritz's shirt from the pile, putting it on her body while everyone grins.

"You're too small for his size," Anaïs remarks.

"Shut up, Heil Hitler." She salutes with her hand to the sounds of laughter.

"Raus, all the Jews out, we will kill all the Jews!" She continues to shout in a German accent to the cheers of the small crowd on the blanket. Everyone looks at her and enjoys the sight of her breasts moving from side to side in the open shirt, barely held by the swimsuit fabric as she waves her hands.

"Juden raus, Juden raus!" She continues to salute with her hand up.

***

My hand is stretched outside the car, feeling the pleasantness of the wind in my fingers as we make our way back to Paris.

"What do you think about Jews?" Ernest asks me, calming his voice while his eyes look ahead to the narrow road.

Is he examining me? Does he suspect me? What should I answer him?

My head turns back for a moment. Everyone is sleeping in the back of the car. Fritz and Fritz with their heads back on the seat, and their mouths open to the afternoon wind. Violette and Anaïs are hugging, each curled up on her Fritz.

"I do not like the Jews, but I don't think they are so dangerous."

"I saw you didn't laugh before when Violette gave her show."

"I used to have a Jewish girlfriend, her name was Sylvie; you couldn't tell she was Jewish."

"What happened to her?"

"We are no longer friends, and I am no longer in Strasbourg."

"I'm not happy about what they're doing to Jews either, but there's no other way to treat them," he continues to speak to me quietly as only the noise of the wind bothers us. "If you understood the economy, you would know how they try to take over the world; they are like a wise fox who wants to break into a vineyard

and plunder the grapes that don't
belong to them."

Oberst Ernest is silent for a
moment, as if trying to figure out
how to explain the Jewish problem
to me more appropriately.

"You see, I do not hate them either,
it's like the hunter does not hate
the fox, he appreciates its wisdom,
but must hunt it; otherwise, it
will harm the crop, destroy the
economy. We must stop them; we
have no choice." He looks at me,
and all I can hear is the tire's noise
on the road, jarring my ears.

"Do you understand what I mean?"
The wind is drying my lips.

"I think I do." I smile at him,
the smile of a good woman
who appreciates an intelligent
explanation but wants to jump out

of the car into the hard asphalt, escape this metal box that takes me forward. Even Dad, who understood economics, did not understand enough about the Germans.

***

"Goodbye, German hero soldiers," Anaïs salutes in a sleepy voice. She tries to grab Fritz's officers' cap, but he pulls her hand away and does not allow it, while Ernest parks the car at the foot of the Arc de Triomphe, hurries out, and approaches to open the door for me.

"I enjoyed your company; you were a perfect companion," he compliments me.

"I enjoyed it too, thank you, thank you for reading me poetry."

"Have we arrived?" Violette asks in a sleepy voice and rises from her Fritz.

"Yes, we are at the Arc de Triomphe," Ernest answers her.

"To our triomphe," says Anaïs.

"Did you forget we won?" Fritz answers her, but she fills his mouth with a passionate farewell kiss.

"This is where we part." Ernest stands politely next to the vehicle, ignoring the rest. I think he expects me to kiss him. What should I do?

"Thanks again for a pleasant day." My hand is outstretched towards him, but I can't get any closer. I'm a Frenchwoman licking German boots, unable to kiss a German officer. I've never kissed a man.

As I start to move away from him, he grabs my hand for a moment, stopping me.

"Mademoiselle Monique."

"Yes, Herr Oberst Ernest?" Will he force me to kiss him?

"Next week, I have to go on a day trip to the North Shore area. Would you like to join me? Just the two of us." And I nod to him in the affirmative, releasing my hand and walking down the boulevard. What else could I answer him?

I'm a French prostitute who will have to kiss a German officer who wants to politely hunt down the Jews.

***

"How was your polite guy?" Lizette asks me when I walk in.

"He invited me on a day trip."

"And will you go with him?" What to tell her?

"I think I'll go, though sometimes I feel like I have to sacrifice part of myself."

"Will you drink coffee with me? Keep me company?"

"Have you ever sacrificed anything?" I ask Lizette as we sit down, and I hold the warm cup in my hands.

"I don't feel it was a sacrifice because I believed in what I was doing."

"And after that, weren't you disappointed in yourself?"

"Why should I be disappointed in myself if I tried my best?"

"I keep on trying, but afterwards I feel disappointed in myself, I so want to succeed."

"Life does not work this way; sometimes life can't even provide us a normal cup of coffee." She smiles at me and places the cup of bitter coffee substitute on the table.

"Thank you for listening to me."

"Thank you, my child, for keeping an old lady company; I think you've sacrificed enough for one evening. It's time for you to go up to your room to sleep." I get up and look at her husband's picture, which is in the silver frame on the fireplace. He stands in his army uniform, looking at me with pride, not knowing that a few days later he will run to his death in front of German machine guns on the Marne front, in that previous great war.

The First Kiss

"Are you waiting for someone?"
Simone asks me a few days after
the picnic.

"No, why?"

"Because you've been looking at
the front door all day."

For several days now, I have been
restless, waiting for Herr Ernest
to enter through the glass door,
feeling tense whenever the doorbell
rings. How would I travel with him
for a whole day? What does he
want from me?

"Sorry, can I have two croissants?"
a soldier asks me in bad French,
and I hurry to serve him.

"Mademoiselle Monique?" Another

soldier in a grey-green uniform approaches Marie, who is cleaning the tables with a damp cloth.

"No, she's there." She points at me over the counter.

"Mademoiselle Monique?"

"Yes, that's me."

"I have a letter for you." And he reaches his hand in a straight motion across the counter, while I move uncomfortably under Simone's scrutiny.

"The commander asked me to wait here for an answer." He speaks French with a German accent, cuts the words sharply before walking to the corner of the store, standing still, waiting for my answer.

"What's in the letter?" asks

Simone, leaving the cash drawer for a moment.

"I don't know," I answer her, blushing and heading to the back room, tearing open the envelope and reading the words written in perfect handwriting, arranged in straight lines.

Dear Mademoiselle Monique,

You are kindly invited to join me for a day tour of northern France, two days from now.

My assistant is waiting for your reply.

Best Regards,

Oberst Ernest

**Commander of the 566
Engineering Brigade**

"Monique, there are customers."
I hear Simone's voice, and I have
to stop looking at Ernest's curly
signature; I hurry back to the
counter while holding the white
paper in my hand.

"Tell him I will join him," I mumble
to his assistant soldier, who has to
get close to hear me.

"I miss the days when French women had dignity," Simone says to Marie a few minutes later, as they chat in the back room. My fingers arrange the remaining pastries on the tray, even though I already finished doing so before Ernest's assistant came in.

What is he expecting of me? I need to talk to someone. Marie passes by, and I think of Claudine. Why did I notice the boy that day?

"Monique, come here please," Simone calls me at the end of the day as I say goodbye to her.

"This is for you, your salary." She puts the green bills in my hands.

"You gave me too much." I return some of the bills to her.

"No, it's yours, you replaced

Claudine, and I decided to give you a raise; you deserve it." And I hurry out into the street, forgetting to thank her. Why didn't I ignore the boy that day?

The boy near the newsstand does not hand me an official letter written on white paper, signed with a curled signature; he doesn't even wait for my answer, he just whispers to me: "Metro Opera." And right after that, he shoves a bundle of newspapers into a big leather bag, and starts running down the street while waving at the newspaper, shouting the news headlines everywhere. "The Americans are invading Italy; the German army has repulsed them in a heroic battle, read about it now in the Paris Soir newspaper."

As I walk towards the Opera, I can

still see the boy running down the street and the people approaching him, paying in coins and taking newspapers from his hand, but my lips are dry and my thoughts are elsewhere; how will Philip react?

***

"What was it like going out with a German officer?" Philip walks around the basement like a panther looking for an exit in the damp walls that close in on us, hardly looking at me. My hands are placed on the wood table, waiting for his, but he keeps on standing, refusing to sit across from me.

"I did not go out with him alone. We all went out for a picnic day at the Marne." He didn't say anything to me when I entered the basement, moving away and not asking how I felt.

"Is it nice to have a picnic on the banks of the Marne? I'll bet the river is quiet and cold in the summer heat; the wind is pleasant; you can lie on the grass in the shade of the trees and laugh." He continues his ugly speech.

"Yes, it is pleasant there."

"And can you still hear the machine guns' nonstop noise, or the cries of the wounded from the previous war against the green-eyed Germans?"

"We did not talk about it."

"Did you enjoy swimming in the river? Cooling your body off from all the heat and sweat?"

"No, I did not enjoy bathing in the cool water."

"Why didn't you enjoy swimming in the river? The German language didn't suit you?"

"Why are you asking me such questions?"

"Because I'm interested and want to know about you, isn't that what we do in our meetings? I ask questions, and you answer them?"

"No, I did not enjoy the water."

"So what did you do? Did you wear a swimsuit, especially for him to see?"

"I did not go into the water."

"Why didn't you go into the water? I heard the German officers enjoyed that their French dates wore swimsuits for them."

"Why are you talking to me like this?"

"Because I want to know who I'm talking to right now."

"I did not bring a swimsuit with me, because I do not have a swimsuit, because I have not worn a swimsuit in years." I get up and push the table away from me.

"Do you think I was interested in going for a bath in the Seine when a day earlier I'd been searching for leftover food in garbage cans? Do you think it matters to me how do I look in a swimsuit? Do you think it's fun to sit in a car with a German officer? To talk with him about the Jews, not knowing if he doesn't like them, or maybe if he raised the subject because he suspects that I am Jewish? Do you think it's such a pleasure to be with someone who scares me and invites me to travel with him alone for a whole day, to try to think what I will do if he tries to kiss me?" I shout the last words and breathe quickly.

"I'm sorry; I did not mean that."

"You meant everything," I sit down in the chair again and cover my face. "Time after time, you send me from this basement to get you more pieces of information."

"I apologize." His arm wraps around me as he leans on the floor next to me, and I feel the smell of his body, with the same aroma of a printing press in his fingers. "Don't cry; I didn't mean to hurt you."

"I don't cry." My hands cover my face; I don't want him to see me like that. "He read me poetry; he asked me if I'd like him to read me poetry."

"I apologize; I love poetry." He lifts me from the concrete floor and hugs my body, his hands pleasant and warm.

"Do you really like poetry?" I look up at him, wanting to believe, feeling his hand stroking my back and not wanting him to stop.

"Yes, once, at the Sorbonne, in another life that will never return." His lips are so close to mine.

"Were you a student at the Sorbonne?" I did not expect his lips to touch mine, but they do.

"A poor student at the Sorbonne."

I cling to him tighter and close my eyes.

What are all these sensations? I can feel the touch of his fingers through the fabric of the dress as I breathe heavily. My hands cling to his shoulders tightly as our lips tighten and keep touching more and more, unable to stop.

"I have to go." My hands push him away, and I move backward, trying to catch my breath as I look into his dark eyes, feeling the rough wall scratching my back.

"I apologize." He's trying to get close to me again.

"Goodbye." I move away from his warm hands and lips, panting up the stairs. I know that if I stay, I won't be able to cross the bridge again to the German Headquarters area and walk as if nothing has changed under the red flags of swastikas fluttering in the evening breeze.

***

I have to stop for a few moments; I'm too excited. I need to talk to someone, someone who will listen to me without me having to lie.

"This is for you, my girl, may a loving man give you a flower."
I place the bouquet on the cold stone and sit down next to her. The old saleswoman at Trocadero Square tried kissing my hand when I bought a huge bouquet, paying her in a pile of bills above the price she asked. Again and again, she thanked me, blessing me with

love while I walked away from her, feeling cleaner without all those green-grey bills in my pocket.

The sun will soon set, and I have to hurry and tell her, before the cemetery gate closes.

"His lips were pleasant to me, but I was stressed. Suddenly I began to breathe heavily." I'm trying to explain it to her.

"I still feel the touch of his hands as they passed over my breasts through my dress." The words come out of my mouth. But I'm too ashamed to tell her about the strange feeling in the bottom of my stomach. I don't want her to think that I am a prostitute who cannot control herself.

"I ran away from him. He said nothing about Oberst Ernest. I should go with him. I did not tell you about Herr Oberst Ernest. I'm so scared."

As I walk out of the cemetery, smiling at the older guard getting ready to lock the gate, I imagine Claudine whispering that I have nothing to fear from Oberst Ernest and that everything will be okay.

Everything will be okay.

***

"Do you feel comfortable?" Herr Oberst Ernest asks as I sit next to him in his army command car's back seat. I can smell the eau de cologne from his shaved face when he leans towards me and helps me arrange my small bag.

This time I waited alone at the foot of the Arc de Triomphe, my body slightly shivering from the autumn's early morning breeze, but precisely at the time we set, I heard an engine roaring from the empty boulevard.

"Guten morgen." Oberst Ernest got out of the bluish-grey car, holding his hand out and helping me get into the back seat while I hold his black glove-wrapped hand. His personal driver sat behind the wheel, ignoring my existence and looking straight ahead like he was welded into place.

"Now you'll be more comfortable." He takes his field binoculars out of side storage, hands it to the driver, and places my bag there instead. "Shall we go?"

The Champs Élysées is empty of cars at this hour, and even on the sidewalk only a few people are walking on their way to work. I look at them and imagine myself walking on the empty boulevard now. Would I look at the passing German vehicle, giving a look of contempt at the woman sitting next to the German officer?

"Should I ask the driver to close the roof?" Oberst Ernest asks me when he notices a shiver gripping me for a moment.

"No, it's okay, I'm not cold." I lie and stare forward at the driver's back, feeling that I deserve contemptuous glances.

"What are you thinking about?"

"The city waking up."

"This city is so special, look at the magnificent building facades, we Germans definitely have something to learn from you." He speaks to me while saluting the guards at the checkpoint in Concord Square. The car slows down as it passes the concrete block and barbed wire barrier, and I look down, wondering if these are the regular guards and whether they recognize me.

"We will make Berlin more beautiful than Paris. The Führer has already approved the plans, a combination of French art and triumphant Prussian spirit." He salutes the Headquarters guards as we pass under the huge swastika flag hanging from the Army Headquarters building, and my fingernails scratch my knees.

"Where are we going?"

"To La Coupole, near the border with Belgium, close to Dunkirk where you grew up. It's a small, unimportant village; you probably know the place." And I try to smile; my eyes are fixed on his black gloves while the driver speeds the vehicle through the quiet streets, turning on Opera Avenue towards the exit north of the city.

"Why are we going there?"

"Military matters that wouldn't interest a beautiful companion like you, you will surely enjoy the open nature and the lovely places we will encounter on our way."

"I haven't been there in such a long time."

"I'm sure you'll be happy to return

to your childhood places; I have made you a small surprise." He smiles at me.

"Surprise?"

"Don't all women like surprises? But in the meantime, you can sit back and relax; we have a long way to go." He approaches me, and again I feel the smell of eau de cologne from his neck as he takes my hand and places it in his leather-gloved palm.

***

"Halt!" Ernest's hand quickly touches the driver's shoulder, and my body tilts forward as the vehicle stops, tires screeching.

"Wait here," he tells me and gets

out of the vehicle, pulling his firearm out of the leather case, and I start shaking.

What happened? Is it about me? I look back at the road, watching him walking slowly, holding the gun in his hand. Is that the surprise for me? Shall I go out of the car and run away? I have to stop shaking.

A pair of grey ears move between the bushes, and a rabbit begins to run across the road while Oberst Ernest raises his hand holding the gun. I look down and close my eyes.

There is no gunshot, but I can't open my eyes, waiting.

"It managed to escape," he tells the driver as he opens the vehicle door, returning the firearm to the leather case.

"It was close." I hear him speak for the first time.

"I'll catch it next time," he smiles at him, signaling with his hand to start driving.

"We will not give up." The driver turns his head for a moment before pressing the accelerator.

"Did you see how it managed to escape?" He takes my hand again. I have to smile.

"I barely got to see it. I did not know you were hunting."

"The military is a profession; hunting is a hobby that every military man with sharp senses adopts for himself." He looks at me. "Are you cold?"

"No, I'm fine."

"You're cold; you're shaking." And he asks the driver to stop and close the roof before we continue down the narrow road. Occasionally we pass a horse pulling the cart of a local farmer or a military truck, but there are no civilian cars on the road, probably because of the lack of fuel.

"You're silent today."

"Sorry, I apologize."

"I thought you'd enjoy visiting the places of your childhood."

Why does he mention it? Why did I agree to travel with him for a day trip?

"I'm sorry, I'm a little hungry."

"Sorry, what a lack of consideration, we've been traveling

for so long and I have not asked you if you had already eaten breakfast." Herr Ernest gives one short command to the driver, and within minutes the vehicle stops at the side of the narrow road, a blanket is pulled out of the trunk, and a picnic basket is placed beside a plowed field.

"The surprise, please join me." Oberst Ernest approaches the vehicle, inviting me to step out, and I watch on all the food arranged just for me on the picnic blanket.

"Is it good for you?"

"The food is delicious, thank you." I watch the fields around us, the ground is waiting for autumn plowing, some trees stand in the distance, and I can feel a pleasant morning breeze. Even though his intentions are good, his gaze makes me nervous, and the meat sandwich gets stuck in my throat, suffocating me.

"Tell me how you got to Paris," he asks, and I finally understand his intention by inviting me to join him. He promised me surprises.

"I thought we would not talk about it." I'm trying to smile at him, but too nervously.

"I thought I would like to know more about a lovely companion joining me on a one-day trip."

"You will not want to hear what happened; it has to do with you, the Germans." But I know I'll have to tell him what happened, this is why he invited me in the first place.

"I would like to hear your story, to know what happened to you."

"It's going to bother you."

"I promise it won't."

"It was three years ago, in the summer, only the wheat had not yet been harvested. The whole field was full of crops." And he looks at me with his green eyes, concentrating on my lips.

"We were running from you." I'm trying to think of the story.

"It was a hot day, the sun was burning my skin, and the road was full of people," I cannot remember the details, his gaze presses me.

"Is that all you remember of your mom and dad?" he asks, and hits his neck, killing a mosquito. What to tell him?

"We were in a neverending convoy," I try to think of Mom and Dad and Jacob, the real ones, not the ones from the story. My eyes close as I concentrate on all the horrible rumors recently coming out about Auschwitz, imagining them walking in front of me in the field, and I start to cry; I miss them so much.

"The road was full of people, and planes came and shot at us, and my father and mother." How did I get to sit for breakfast with a German officer instead of being with my family?

"I'm sorry that happened to you. It shouldn't have happened." He hands me a handkerchief. "I did not know that was what had happened to them."

"You couldn't know." I take the handkerchief from him and wipe my eyes; what happened to them?

"It is terrible what happened to the French people in this war; you shouldn't have declared war on us, forcing us to conquer you. You are such a culture-loving nation; there could be great friendship between us."

"I haven't left Paris since." I return the handkerchief to him. Herr Ernest takes it in silence and continues to look at me.

"And why did you agree to go out with a German officer after all that happened to you?" A feeling of cold surrounds me as the ground drops beneath my feet, what can I tell him? My fingers tap the picnic blanket nervously.

"I cried for two years. I don't want to cry anymore; I want to live. I want to be on the side that talks about art, the side that has a purpose, I know the Germans are good people and that my parents died by mistake. Mistakes happen in war." Why couldn't I remember the story as I practiced it so many times?

"Yes, mistakes happen in war." Ernest relaxes back and sips the sweet drink, looking at me while nodding.

"Shall we continue on our way?" he suggests, and I relax, getting up and straightening my dress as he signals the driver to approach. "Will you take a picture of us?"

"A little souvenir from a day of fun," he tells me in his quiet voice as we both stand in front of the driver, and I think I've passed his test.

"Smile, he is pointing the camera at us." His hand hugs my waist as he gets me closer, and I feel the softness of the leather glove, which he put on his hand again, ready for the drive to continue.

"Magnificent." He smiles at the driver after he took our photo. "We've almost arrived."

***

"La Coupole" is written in German on the white road sign, and it is already the third military checkpoint we have passed in the last minutes, each more strict than its predecessors. The soldiers carefully examine us, saluting as they see Oberst Ernest.

"I need you to wait for me here. I have to see something, feel free to walk around," he tells me as the driver parks the vehicle on the side of the road so as not to disturb the concrete trucks that pass us.

"When will you return?"

"It's going to take me about an hour." He smiles at me before disappearing with the driver behind the hill, leaving me by myself in the vehicle.

It's nice to be alone for some time, breathing the free air, lying in the back seat and looking at the clouds in the sky or standing and looking around, searching for something to do with myself; I have an hour.

***

"TOP SECRET." It is written on the brown cardboard folder placed on the vehicle's front seat, in elegant black writing in the German language, with the stamp of an eagle spreading its wings, holding a swastika in its claws. They must have left it here by mistake as they organized the documents. For a few minutes now, I've been watching it apprehensively.

Although Philip warned me not to risk myself, this is my chance. I can bring him the real material he is so looking for, not just gossip from soldiers in their free time in Paris. My feet carry me around the car, checking that there is no other person or soldier nearby, only the trucks and tiny soldiers are visible in the distance, but they are far away. The trees hide the massive building under construction, and there is no German soldier nearby.

It's now or never. I must take advantage of their mistake, making Philip proud of me at least once; it's no time to be afraid now; all I need is a few minutes. My hand searches for paper and a pencil from my bag.

"What are you doing, what are you writing?"

"Nothing." I quickly get up behind the vehicle and straighten my dress, hiding the papers behind my back; the pencil is left tossed among the weeds.

"Show me that." Oberst Ernest stands in front of me, speaking quietly, the German language coming out of his mouth like a snake's hiss. His driver is standing next to him, holding the brown leather briefcase and binoculars.

"I'm not doing anything, just sitting outside the car."

"What do you have in hand? Show me your hands, both of them."

"It's nothing, just something I was writing."

"I thought we had a great friendship," his mouth whispers the words with a bitter smile as his black hand waits to receive what I'm holding.

My hands reach out to him slowly, handing him the wrinkled papers I hold in my fist.

"What is this?" he asks as he carefully examines the crumpled papers.

"Flowers."

"What are these flower drawings? Nothing is written here."

"Drawings of flowers."

"Why are you drawing flowers?"

"I was bored and delayed, so I got out of the car and sat down in the grass, drawing flowers, I like to draw flowers." Oberst Ernest looks for another moment at the papers gripped in his black leather gloves, and silently returns them to me. While I debate whether to say something, he walks away with the driver following him and turns to him, but I cannot hear their talking. My hand is on my stomach.

On the way back to Paris, everything returns to the way it used to be. Herr Ernest politely gives me a hand to help me get in the car and asks if I'm comfortable. As we turn onto the road towards Paris, he continues to talk about art and the Louvre Palace, and how special it would be to visit it. Still, I have a hard time listening to him and paying attention to the conversation. Most of the time my eyes are on the back of the driver who is driving in silence. What would have happened to me if I had not noticed the open binocular case left under the glove compartment? What would have happened if I had not thought of the grey rabbit that crossed the road?

My stomach hurts, and I try to close my eyes and breathe slowly, imagining what it is like to run through the wood, escaping from the hunter.

***

"We have arrived." I open my eyes in the darkness to the touch of a leather glove on my cheek, looking at the silhouette of a German officer leaning over me, and I want to scream.

"Mademoiselle Monique, we have arrived, wake up." The German officer whispers to me. It's Oberst Ernest, and I'm inside his military car. From the window, I can notice the Arc de Triomphe standing in the dark above us.

"Give me your hand." I grab his palm and stand in the street, getting used to the streetlights' dim lights, only a few of them shining due to war regulations, and the square deserted in the late hour.

"You were cold, so I covered you with my coat." I slowly look down and examine the heavy coat that covers my body, making me warm, realizing I'm wearing a Nazi German officer's uniform. My fingers slide slowly over the black metal cross close to my chest, feeling the tip of the blades.

"Thank you for taking care of me."

"Thank you so much for a fascinating day." He does not mention a word of what happened at the construction site.

"Thank you." I do not mention it either.

"I would be glad to meet you again."

"I would be glad to be your companion."

His hands grip my neck as he brings my face closer to his lips, pinning them to his. Despite the day's travel, I can still smell the eau de cologne from his cheeks as he pulls me closer while his tongue penetrates my lips.

My hands rest on the sides of my body while his tongue touches mine until he stops, and in the gloom of the evening, I can see him smiling.

"I'm glad we kissed," he says. What does it matter what I answer? He would have done it anyway. He's used to getting what he wants.

"I'm glad we kissed too."

"May I? Please." He raises his hand.

"What?" I ask him, not understanding.

"My military coat, can I have it?"

"Sorry." I take off the coat and hand him the grey-green cloth, feeling the evening's cold.

"Good night, Mademoiselle Monique."

"Good night, Herr Oberst Ernest."

My eyes follow the military vehicle moving down the almost-deserted boulevard, smelling the burnt petrol it's left behind and starting to walk home. The sleepy French policeman who guards the Arc de Triomphe monster follows me with his gaze, but I ignore him, directing my steps towards the single lit streetlight at the alley's end.

I need someone to hug me very much.

***

I count the stairs down the dirty basement in the Latin Quarter, waiting to hug him. So much has happened since the last time we met, when we kissed, and I'm so ashamed of myself. I kissed a German officer.

Philip stands waiting for me at the bottom of the stairs, as always, but when I approach him and try to hold his hands, he steps back.

"Monique, I apologize for what happened last time; it should not have happened."

I get closer and look at his dark eyes, examining them closely. Are they brown or black?

"I shouldn't have kissed you," he continues to strike me. "It is too dangerous for us; we have a mission to do."

"Yes, we have a mission to do." I turn my back on him and go to the wooden table, sitting down in the chair, wanting him to stay away from me. I will survive, even without his hug. Philip approaches me and looks for more to say, but I no longer look into his eyes, instead carefully examining the grooves in the old table's wooden surface.

"They're building something big in the north. I don't know what it is."

"Did you hear what I said? We are at war, I'm sorry." He grabs my arm and tries to pull me towards him.

"There are a lot of army checkpoints, a lot of soldiers." I pull my hand away from him and sit down again, not wanting him to touch me.

"It's just not the right time. We're at war." He sits in front of me and places his hands on the table, and

I look closely at the black color spots on his fingers, but I don't put my fingers on his.

"A lot of concrete trucks, maybe a big bunker."

"I am not allowed to do what I did. It endangers us and our judgment. Last time never happened."

"And he kept talking to me about art; did your Sorbonne never happen either?"

"You have to forget about the Sorbonne; my Sorbonne belongs to another life, it's not me anymore, now it's me and you here in a shabby basement in the Latin Quarter in an occupied and hungry city."

"He took an interest and asked me about my past." You don't really know what it is to be hungry.

"Did he suspect you? I do not want you to risk yourself." He puts his hands on mine.

"I didn't risk myself, and he doesn't suspect me at all. He treated me very nicely. He is not a poor student." I take my hands off the table.

"Did you see some documents? You need to be careful not to get close to the documents; it might be a trap."

"No, nothing, just the trucks, and one rabbit running across the road."

"I do not want you to get hurt."

"I will not get hurt, I know how to take care of myself, we even took pictures together, he has a picture of both of us. I think you should get me a camera next time we go, so I can take pictures too." At least someone will have a souvenir from me.

"Did you take a picture with him? Why do you need a camera? It's dangerous."

"Because if I had a camera, I could take pictures of the bunker they are building." And also get caught and be executed, maybe that's what happens to one like me who kissed two men. You regret it and say it never happened, and the other is a German officer.

"I'm not bringing you a camera, it's too dangerous. Why did he photograph you?"

"Because he wanted to have a

souvenir from our trip, of the one he kissed." Or the one he is trying to hunt.

"Did you kiss him back?" His hand is no longer on the table, he gets up and walks around the room, and I look again at the wooden grooves on the table, examining them carefully.

"You should check what's up there in the north. I think he's a senior commander." And he did not say it was a mistake, as you said. You do not even want to sit at the same table with me.

"You have to be careful of him, he's dangerous."

"We have to take risks, don't we? Aren't we at war?" I get up to go, and he repeats our traditional blessing.

"Take care of yourself."

"Take care of yourself," I answer before turning around and walking away. Slowly I climb the stairs leading out into the street, hating him and those words.

"Take care of yourself, you miserable Frenchie," I repeat the blessing the following nights before I fall asleep, trying to forget what his lips tasted like when he kissed me in the basement that time. It never happened. He will not embrace me anymore. I need to learn to stay away from him.

***

Invitation

It takes a while until I turn my attention to the next soldier in line, handing him the bag full of cookies, raising my head, looking into his green eyes, and freezing.

"I thought you used to send your assistant." Despite the showcase that separates us, I can smell his eau de cologne.

"I wanted to come and see the place where you work, the place everyone is talking about." He ignores the rudeness of my words while Simone closes the cash register and tries to listen, making herself busy.

"I work here when you don't surprise me." I show him the small space, full of chairs, tables, and cigarette smoke, trying to pull myself together while ignoring Simone as she bends to take something out of the counter but stays close.

"So you don't like to be surprised?"

"Not really."

"I don't like to be surprised either; I think we just found another thing in common." He smiles at me, and I manage to smile back.

"Sorry, Madame," he turns to Simone in French as she rises, smiling at the sight of his many ranks and decorations, as she first noticed him. "Can I borrow Mademoiselle Monique from you? I'd be happy if she could show me around the city."

"She'll be happy to join you." She smiles at him and nods at me to leave, and I turn to remove the apron around my waist, wondering what words Simone will use after I walk out the door. Will she tell Marie that she misses the respectable young French women? Those who can't be found in the city anymore?

"Thank you very much; she will get back to you tomorrow." He thanks Simone while opening the boulangerie door for me, putting his arm around my waist. We both know I am his property, what surprise has he arranged for me today?

***

"Is everything okay? Why are we getting inside?" I break the silence between us in front of the Tuileries Gardens' gate.

"I have a few hours, and I wanted to spend some time with you." Oberst Ernest stands at the sign to the garden entrance, pinned to the open iron gate: "Entry to Jews is forbidden." Left over from those days when there were still Jews in this city.

"I thought you wanted me to show you the city."

"Isn't this garden a beautiful part of the city?" He crosses the gate and steps inside while his boots crush the white gravel.

"What did you do in the army before you knew me?" I hesitate for a split-second but walk after him into the garden I have not visited in recent years. The round pool at the entrance is empty of water, and no one sits on the green iron chairs. Where did the marble sculptures go?

"I told you before, I do not want to talk about the East, it will not interest you. When I'm with you, I want to talk about Paris and art, not about the war."

"Why me?"

It takes him a while to answer, as if he is trying to think of the right words. Silently we walk in the almost-empty garden, listening to the noise of gravel under our feet.

"Because you are different, you are not like the others."

He folds his hands behind his back,

looking at the Louvre Palace's vast expanse. "You are quiet, not loud like Violette or disrespectful like Anaïs, you are not trying to impress me, but you are willing to learn. Maybe you are like the French nation, lying in wait for someone to come and take you. And I'm going to be that someone." He smiles to himself at finding the words he was looking for, stopping and looking at me.

"Am I a symbol for the French nation? Triumph and victory?"

"Don't forget who you are; you were born in German Strasbourg, you are only called French because of a historical insult."

"I never forget who I am." I speak German and French, I also kissed him, and I also lick German boots.

"It's only fair that this palace belongs to us. It fills me with pride." He looks around at the Louvre's enormous wings surrounding us, while I wait patiently by his side.

This time, he does not try to kiss me or even give me a hand. Herr Ernest keeps walking towards the exit from the garden, as if stating that from now on, I belong to him, and I will continue to follow in his footsteps. The marble sculptures of the garden peek at me from the corner by the wall, they were taken out and moved, gathered together and wrapped in sandbags, probably for protection from air bombs, I wonder if they too would like to be somewhere else.

The small gravel is trampled under my shoes at the gate's exit and the sign: "Jews are not allowed."

"Let me invite you for cake on the avenue," he tells me, and I obediently follow.

***

"Do you like the cake?"

"The cake is delicious; thank you."

I look down at the plate in front of me, filled with a slice of sweet cake made of real sugar, careful not to raise my eyes to the avenue and the people passing us. Oberst Ernest leans back as he watches me, savoring a glass of champagne from a chilled bottle which stands in special silverware beside the table. Why has no one taught me how to behave with a man who invites me to champagne?

"You need to wear bright dresses; it will suit you."

"Thank you; I'll try."

"Since when do you draw flowers? Like then, on our trip?" He mentions that day for the first time, and I tense up.

"Ever since I was little."

"In Paris?"

"Yes."

"I thought you grew up in Strasbourg."

"I grew up in Strasbourg, but I received my first drawing notebook from Paris, Dad bought it for me in Paris, on one of his work trips."

I carefully bite the cake, trying to stay calm. I must not make such a stupid mistake again, ever.

"To your flower drawings." He raises the glass in my honor, and I smile, tapping my glass against his, hoping he has not noticed my trembling fingers.

"Halt." Herr Ernest shout-whispers as he leaps from his chair, and I freeze in my seat. All the people in the café stop talking and look at us. Only the sound of a fork falling on the sidewalk breaks the silence, disturbed by the sound of Ernest's spiked boots.

"Halt!" He walks and places his hand on the back of a man who is walking down the street. The man stops and looks at him with a surprised look.

"What did you do?" Oberst Ernest stands above him, getting closer to the man's face.

"I didn't do anything," the man answers him in a weeping voice.

"Apologize to the lady." He leads him with his head lowered, slapping him on the floor at my feet.

"Apologize to the lady for spitting on the sidewalk."

"I apologize." He cries at my feet, and I look down but close my eyes so as not to see him and burst into tears.

"Do you accept the apology?"

Yes, I nod to Herr Ernest.

"Get out of here, filthy Frenchman." He picks him up by the back of his head and pushes him from the table area back into the street. The man walks away quickly, not looking back, and my gaze follows him until he disappears among the passersby, becoming a blur.

Only then do I let my eyes wander around, seeing all the people who have been watching us start talking again. The waiters are running once more between the tables, and the noise of conversation fills the air. Even the small crowd that gathered on the street disappears as if it never happened.

"I apologize for what happened." Oberst Ernest sits back in his chair, picking his officers' hat up off the floor and placing it back on the table, where it was before everything started.

"Nothing happened," I manage to say something, looking at the sugar cake on my plate.

"They should be taught the meaning of respect." He looks around, and all the people of the café stop their stolen glances in our direction, returning to their small talk.

"I forgave him; he did not mean to."

"Do you like the cake?"

"Yes, very much, thank you." How can he think of the cake now?

"We didn't propose a toast properly." Herr Ernest again raises his glass in the air, and we tap our glasses again, before I bring the glass to my lips, drinking it all and ignoring the bitter taste of champagne.

Towards the evening he accompanies me down the avenue as I stare at the sidewalk, strolling beside him.

"I live in a hotel. Unfortunately, it is not appropriate for me to invite a companion to visit my room." I nod in silence and breathe a sigh of relief.

"But I would love to meet you again." He holds my neck and brings me closer to a kiss. His lips touch mine again, and his tongue penetrates my mouth before he says goodbye to me and I turn back home, hating myself a little more, the smell of eau de cologne staying in my nose.

The key's sound is the only noise I hear when I enter the dark apartment, passing through the dim living room and climbing into my attic. Lizette told me she would be out, and I am left with my private darkness within the four walls and the simple iron bed.

"Dear God," the words of prayer are carried as I lie in bed and look at the black ceiling, "please turn everything back; please turn all that has happened into a bad dream. Please return me to my house; I promise I will not quarrel with Mom anymore when she asks me to keep an eye on Jacob, please. I promise to be the best I can be."

But the next morning, I wake up in the same attic, without Mom's voice hurrying me to go stand in line for bread, and Lizette asks me if I'll drink coffee with her after I'm done tidying up the house. And I do not hear the sounds of Jacob's laughter and Dad reading the newspaper, explaining to Mom that even though the situation is tense, no war will break out.

The autumn rain does not stop on my way to work, wetting the fallen leaves on the street. And the Nazi flag on Rivoli Street, at the German headquarters, drips a trickle of cold water on my head as I cross the grey street below.

He is no different from the others when he enters the boulangerie in his grey-green uniform. He closes the door behind him and shakes his coat from the raindrops that have been falling since the morning, looking for me with his eyes, like many others.

"Mademoiselle Monique?" He turns to me, ignoring Simone and her disapproving looks.

"Yes, that's me." My eyes look at him in surprise; how does he know my name?

"This is a present from Herr Oberst Ernest." He places a package wrapped in purple tissue paper on the counter, clicking his boots as if preparing to salute me, and turns and leaves the store, gently closing the door behind him.

"Who is it from?" Simone asks and approaches me, as if to make it clear that she is in charge here and that I have to get her approval before taking the package from the courier, even though she was standing next to me and heard what the soldier said.

"From him." I'm trying to calm myself.

"And what's in the package?"

"I don't know." I hold it tightly in my hands, afraid she will snatch it and tear away the paper, determined to find out what present I've received from a German officer.

"Then open it."

My hands begin to unravel the white ribbon that envelops the package; my smile makes me feel guilty.

"Are you opening it?"

What has he sent me? And what if it's an intimate item, as I saw that time in the window of the shop with Violette? I hurry to the back room, sitting in the corner on a wooden crate where no one can see. What if he expects something from me? With a trembling hand, I remove the purple tissue paper, feeling its delicacy between my fingers.

"Marie, please call Monique, decent French women should not receive a foreign man's gift." But I ignore her.

My hands grip the fancy notebook, wrapped in a hardcover of black leather with the curved letter 'E' engraved, and I can feel it as I run my finger over the smooth leather.

"Monique, there's a customer."

426

I open the notebook and hold the white note, written in rounded handwriting.

"To Monique,

Have a diary to draw as many flowers as you wish.

I would be happy if you would join me on a two-day trip to Normandy two weeks from today, keeping me company, including an overnight stay at a hotel.

Herr Oberst Ernest."

"Monique, the customer is waiting."

I look at the note for another moment before I return it between the diary pages, shove it into my bag that hangs on the hanger behind the door, and hurry back to my place by the counter.

On the way home I stroll, wanting to get wet in the rain, feeling I deserve to suffer. Why did I smile more than I did on my birthday two years ago? When I received a box of chocolate from Mom?

Again Lizette is not there, and the house is empty, and I step into the cold attic. What does Oberst Ernest expect me to do? Is it that thing I'm so afraid of?

***

"What do you expect me to do?" I yell at Philip a few days later.

"I expect you to do your best," he answers me angrily as he gets up from the chair, moving it rudely.

"I promise to do my best," I answer him, and look at the simple cardboard notebook that lies between us on the wooden table, wondering why we started fighting at all.

I did not plan to hug him as I went down the stairs to the basement, I promised myself I'd get over him, but my hands couldn't stop themselves. I embraced his body, holding on so tightly and smelling his body odor, mixed with the smell of gun oil, unable to release him.

"Just one moment," I whispered to him, "I know we must not." And he hugs me in silence, enfolding my back with his hands, and stroking me gently.

"I brought you something," he whispers to me, and I hug him even harder.

"One more moment."

"Just to let you know, they liked the information you gave us the previous time." He keeps stroking me, and I can't stop clinging to his warm body, feeling my whole body like electricity; what are these feelings?

"Who wants me to know?" I'm thinking about his fingers caressing my back.

"The ones who got the information. We must stop; we said it never happened." And I release my hands and back up; it never happened again.

"Can I start my report now?" He doesn't even want to hug me from time to time.

"I brought you something." He pulls out a simple cardboard notebook, placing it on the table.

"What is it?"

"It's a regular notebook. You can write down secret information there. I'll teach you how to hide it between ordinary words so that whoever reads it will not understand that there is information hidden in it." Why is he moving away from me?

The notebook is on the table between us, wrapped in a rough cardboard cover, and rubbed in the corners as if used by someone else before me. Still, I dare not ask, although when I open it, I can see that several pages have been torn from it, and no greeting note is written on the first page.

"Thanks." Shall I tell him about the gift I received from Oberst Ernest?

"He wants to take me with him to Normandy."

"Who, your officer?" And I nod in silence and try to get closer to him, but Phillip walks away from me, sitting down in the wooden chair, looking at me.

"It's a good sign that he trusts you." That's all he says, why isn't he telling me something else?

"What should I do? Tell me what to do."

"You have to go with him," he answers me in a distant voice.

"I'll go with him. I have no choice."

"Maybe I really need to get you a camera so that you can take some pictures."

"Then bring me a camera." I stand up and get ready to go; please stop me from going.

"I apologize; I didn't mean what I said." Philip also stands up and looks at me, but I look aside and panic.

For a moment, it seemed to me that the silhouette of Oberst Ernest was standing in the dark corner of the cellar, watching us, wearing his green-grey uniform with the Iron Cross on his chest.

"What happened?" Philip turns around quickly, his hand already holding the grip of his firearm, ready to pull it out.

"For a moment, I got scared by the pile of pipes in the corner." And Philip looks at me again, his hands releasing his grip on his firearm.

"I worry about you." He softens his voice.

"What do you expect me to do?" I yell at him, still thinking about the basement corner.

"I expect you to do your best," Philip yells at me back.

"I promise to be the best I can be." My hands grip the simple notebook lying on the table between us, and I toss it towards him. "I already have one notebook, from the one who reads me poetry."

"From him?" he asks quietly, and gently grabs the old notebook, stroking it with his fingers.

"It doesn't matter."

And all this time, Oberst Ernest continues to stand in the corner, watching me while his green eyes twinkle under his officers' hat's visor.

"Let's go back and sit."

"I have to go. Get me a camera, that's how I'll be the best I can be."

He's trying to catch and hug me, but I cannot feel his touch when I keep imagining Oberst Ernest watching us. I have to get out of here; I hate this basement.

"Monique, I did not mean it; don't leave angry," I hear him say as I climb the stairs, and I regret that I told him about Oberst Ernest's gift, but I can't return to pick up the old notebook. I also did not tell him that we were going for two days; what would I do when Oberst Ernest wants me to get into his bed?

"Monique, I care about you." He runs up the stairs after me and hugs me tightly, but after a moment, I release his warm hands, continuing on my way out into the alley. He will not be able to understand.

"You probably can't help me with that."

***

"Come to me if you ever need help," she'd told me one of the times the three of us walked together, standing at Pont des Arts and watching the river flow leisurely beneath us.

"I will," I'd answered her at that time, not believing it would happen. What was she thinking of me, I thought while looking at her with combined feelings of reluctance and admiration. My gaze followed her as she leaned against the metal railing and blew the cigarette smoke upwards, ignoring the judgmental looks of passersby towards a smoking woman.

"You might learn something," she'd added, throwing the cigarette into the green-grey river.

And even though I feel that she

was disrespecting me, I have
no other choice, and I leave the
boulangerie in the middle of the
day, promising Simone I won't
take long. I'm not sure Violette can
help me, and I'm ashamed to ask
Lizette, so I find myself walking
down the main avenue near the
Gallery Lafayette store, looking
up at the fancy building numbers,
searching for her workplace.

"Please wait here," the girl at
reception orders while checking my
simple dress, making me feel like a
maid who happened to be here and
would soon be expelled in disgrace.

"Don't pay attention to her."
Anaïs arrives and grabs my
arm, taking me to a room at
the back. "Distinguished ladies
from Germany came to our
fashion house to buy the autumn

collection, and she doesn't want them to feel like they're in the ordinary world." And I do not know if she is trying to encourage me or again insult and patronize me.

The back room is loaded with rolls of colorful fabrics in shades of cream, red and black, and when we are silent, I can hear the conversation in the next room with the German buyer looking for an evening gown for prom.

"She is the wife of a senior officer," Anaïs whispers to me in a contemptuous tone, "She came here specially, from Berlin. In a few days, he will take her to a concert at the opera wearing a dress we sewed for her, and she has no idea that her husband brought his mistress here a week ago, buying her several dresses."

"I don't want to disturb you at work."

"You are not disturbing me; there are so many seamstresses around her that they will not notice I've disappeared for a few minutes. They are hovering around all the time, 'Frau' and 'Frau' and 'Frau,' showing her one dress after another."

"Shhhh… they will hear us."

"Do not worry, they are full of admiration for the suspenders that are in fashion again this year; soon they will sell her a new morning dress."

"Don't you like them?"

"I like them a lot. They are providing work to Anaïs and access to fashionable clothes." She smiles as she takes a pack of cigarettes out of her work apron pocket and lights one for herself, not before offering one to me, but I refuse.

"So why did you come to visit?" She blows the smoke and looks at me. "You probably did not just come to talk or see a new outfit." And again, I do not know if she is towering over me.

"Herr Oberst Ernest."

"What about him?"

"I think he expects something from me."

"What?"

"Well... that thing." I approach and whisper to her. "I think he wants it."

"Getting into your panties?"

"I think." I can feel I am blushing.

"I think you're too innocent for all these things."

"I don't know what to do."

"And why did you come to me?" She blows the smoke again up, enjoying humiliating me a little more.

"Because I do not know who to ask, and I thought maybe you know." Why am I blushing?

"Anaïs will teach you." She smiles and grabs my hand, taking me with her through the reception down the marble stairs to the street, ignoring the receptionist who asks her where she is going.

"First of all, you need classy lingerie." She critically looks at me as she reviews my simple dress, alluding to the underwear I'm wearing, while we both stand outside a fancy store of bras and panties.

"Wait," I hold her hand, preventing her from entering the store and embarrassed of myself. "What should I do with him? Shall I refuse him? Agree? What do you do when...?"

"You're so innocent," she looks at me with pity before she takes my hand and enters the store with me. "Do you really think you can refuse him?"

***

After we leave the store, she takes me to a café; I think it's out of pity, and I try not to think about the delicate feeling of the bra and the garter belt, the ones the saleswoman measured on me in the store.

"Does it feel good?" I finally find the courage to come up with the question that scares me.

"Sometimes it's pleasant, and sometimes it's not," she answers me honestly, "but it should not be pleasant, it should serve your goals."

"And what are my goals?"

"Let him be satisfied; if he is satisfied, he will give you what you want."

"And how do I know what to do?"

"Don't worry, he already knows, you're probably not his first." And I blush again.

"Is that how all men are?"

"Yeah, everyone's like that, they just want one thing," she answers me indifferently. What about Philip? Has he already gotten into other girls' panties? Does he even care about me?

"And what about you? Doesn't it bother you?"

"Doesn't what bother me?"

"To be with him when he is a..." And I cannot finish the sentence.

"German?"

Yes, I nod. "Doesn't that worry you?"

"Anaïs has to take care of Anaïs,"
she places the coffee on the table
and continues talking, showing me
at a glance all the German officers
sitting around us eating and
drinking in the magnificent café,
which overlooks the Opera House.
"No one asked me whether to start
this war, and no one asked me how
I was going to get food, so no one
should ask me what I am going to
do to survive."

I try to sip my coffee, but it tastes
bitter to me, even though it's real.

"Do not worry," she puts her hand
on mine, "you will be fine. Wear
what you bought, lie on your
back and let him do the work,
everything will be fine."

"Yeah, I'll let him get into my
panties." I bring my head closer to

her and whisper, trying to speak bluntly and sound mature, but the words sound ugly to me.

"Just like that." She smiles at me, and also at two German officers sitting at a nearby table, looking at us with interest.

"What took you so long?" Simone asks me as I walk through the glass door, looking hostile at the shopping bag I'm trying to hide behind my back. "You said you were going out for a few minutes."

"I apologize, I had to help a friend with a difficult problem."

I will apologize to him for the last time; I need him to hold me before the two-day trip.

The guards on the Pont Neuf bridge ignore me as I pass on my way to the Latin Quarter. I need him to promise me that he will forgive what I intend to do, and never ask me about it.

I'm almost running into his arms, lowering my eyes so as not to stumble on that broken step right in front of the basement entrance. But when my eyes return to look for him, I stop abruptly, trying to walk leisurely again like a young woman.

Philip stands in his same position as always, his body ready to jump towards any noise, but his arms are on his hips, and he does not approach me.

"Monique, meet Robert." He introduces the man standing next to him.

I reach out my hand, embarrassed by his unexpected presence, and tries to breathe as usual. Why is he here? Why today?

"Nice to meet you, Monique."

"Nice to meet you, Robert."

"Sit down," Philip instructs me, and remains standing as the stranger sits in front of me, looking at me for a moment with interest and appreciation. Where to place my hands? On the table? Who is he anyway? What was his name? He's older than the two of us, about thirty years old; what is that brown leather bag hanging over his shoulder?

"Does she know that they will execute her if they catch her?" He turns to Philip standing next to him, keeping distance from me.

"Yes, she knows."

"And she still wants to do it?"

"She asked."

"Are you sure about that?" He finally turns to me, and I'm not sure what exactly he means by that.

"Yes, I'm sure."

"Well," he sighs and opens the leather bag which rests on his shoulder, pulling out a small metal box with buttons and a glass lens, placing it on the table between us. I reach out, and for the first time in my life, I'm holding a camera.

"Carefully, pick it up carefully." He speaks as my fingers glide over the magic of black metal and golden buttons.

"This is a Leica camera, small and compact, the best in the market. There is no substitute for the Germans when it comes to cameras." He sighed, and my fingernails gently scratched the eagle with the swastika engraved on the camera's iron body, feeling reluctant and nauseous. I have to put it back on the table, but I can't; I can't withdraw now, after he arranged a camera for me.

"Now listen, and listen well," Robert demands my attention, "there is no room for mistakes." And in the next minutes, he explains to me about photography, explaining the buttons, how to aim and where to click, what is a film, and how to load it, forcing me to stand and practice.

"You have to aim fast and shoot fast; you have to practice sliding the camera into a hiding place in your bag. You should also have a cover story, at least a basic one, although it won't help you if a German soldier catches you."

He keeps talking to me fluently as I stand in the small basement and turn the camera on, looking at Philip through the viewfinder, pressing the button, and getting used to the noise of the camera shutter opening and closing. Throughout all this time, Philip stands motionless in the room's gloom, looking at Robert and me, not intervening or uttering a word. He trusts me, I can no longer disappoint him, even though I want to change my mind about the whole thing. What did I bring down on myself?

"Monique, you can still change your mind; this camera could be your death sentence." Robert stops me when the tutorial is over, and I hold the camera and understand that it is my most precious possession from now on.

"Monique, you can still back out."

I'm trying to figure out how to hide it in my side bag and looking at Philip. What does he expect me to do? His dark eyes look at me from a distance. Why did I yell at him last time?

"I know it's dangerous," I answer Robert and shove the camera into the bag, trying to give my voice a tone of confidence, but my body trembles with fear. What happens if I fail or make a mistake? Will I let him down? What will happen if they catch me? Why does Robert not leave us alone?

Although I thanked him twice, he stayed to talk to us about cameras and photography, telling us that now he must only take pictures in secret and that he misses the days when he walked the streets and just photographed people.

'Go already,' I whisper to him over and over in my heart, but he does not hear as time goes by, and in the end I have no choice, and I have to say goodbye to them, feeling sad for leaving.

"Take care of yourself," Philip tells me with distant politeness, and Robert joins in too.

"Take care of yourself."

One tear flows from my eyes as I walk out into the narrow alley and look around. I could not apologize to him. The hug will have to wait for next time, if there will be a next time.

Normandy

Despite the coat I'm wearing, the cold of autumn makes me tremble as I wait for Herr Ernest in Place de l'Étoile, shifting my body weight from foot to foot and rubbing my hands.

The Arc de Triomphe monument standing above makes me feel that every time I stand like this in the square, waiting for the German car, the figures engraved on the marble monument despise me more, judging me with tormented looks.

The grey car arrives just in time for me, and Oberst Ernest gets out of it quickly, even ahead of the driver who hurries to open the door for me and stand up straight on the sidewalk.

"Let me." Oberst Ernest takes the travel bag I am holding in my hands, caresses my arm for a moment, and does not forget to compliment me on the dress I am wearing, the one Lizette helped me choose.

The night before, we'd packed the bag together for the two-day trip; I looked in the closet, and Lizette volunteered to help. I'd folded the clothes with a shaking hand, trying not to talk or lie to her.

"Did your girlfriend invite you to come sleep with her tomorrow after work?"

"Yes, she wants us to go out."

"Only one night?"

"Yes."

"And you love him?" She feels I'm not telling the truth.

"Yes."

"So why are you so worried?"

If only I could tell her, or change the characters, I was looking for the right words, but the fear that I'd slip up made me silent, as I tried to fold the same shirt over and over again.

"Give it to me." She smiled and took the bright button shirt from my hand. I did not want to hurt her; she was so important to me; she did not deserve it.

What will I do when Oberst Ernest tries to do it with me? Maybe I can imagine Philip in his place? My fingers tremble as I fold the white lace underwear, carefully placing it at the bottom of the bag over a pair of silk tights, which are so rare because of the war. Anaïs handed them to me. "A gift from me," she'd whispered as she entered the boulangerie for a moment, taking me into a corner and ignoring Simone's gaze. "A woman should look her best." She giggled and placed the soft bundle in my palm, and I had no choice but to thank her and quickly tuck them into my apron pocket, trying not to think what they were meant for.

Occasionally, when the boulangerie was empty of German soldiers, I put my hand in my pocket, feeling the delicate silk in my fingers and trying to ignore the dull pain in the bottom of my stomach.

Everything would be okay, I tried to convince myself, but the inconvenience continued even in the evening as we packed the bag by candlelight. Lately, the power outages in the city have been increasing.

"Take this dress; it's going to fit you." She pulled a warm grey dress out of my closet for the ride.

"How did you know when it was the right time?" I'd held the dress and checked myself in front of the mirror.

"I didn't know; you can never know when it's the right time."

"So when did you decide?"

"I didn't decide, I wanted to," she paused for a moment and lowered her head, "but I wanted it to be special for us, I wanted us to wait until we got married, I thought we should create a moment for us to remember forever.

But he had to join the army; there is always a war or something to fight about. So I told him we'd wait until he came back. Here, that skirt will suit you, too." She put on a dark burgundy skirt, and I thought of the man in the picture waiting for the right moment, so sorry for the last time, for the arrival of Robert, for not kissing him, for not waiting a few more minutes, even though it was already late.

"Do not be sad," Lizette put her hand on my arm, "it's just one story of an old woman, your man is waiting for you, you should be happy."

***

While the grey-blue vehicle heads its way west along the Seine river, Oberst Ernest notices that I'm cold despite the coat on my body, and instructs the driver to stop at the side of the road to close the tarpaulin roof. Quietly I sit in the car and look up at the tarpaulin, slowly closing us into the gloom.

"Now you will be more pleasant."

"Thank you; I love autumn."

"I like the grey color too. I told you we are alike." He smiles at me, and I smile back, concentrating on the big trees. Their yellow leaves are falling on the wet road, and I try to ignore his hand wrapped in his black glove, resting on my thighs.

"I brought you the poetry book you love, for the evening at the hotel."

462

"Thank you; I'd enjoy listening to you."

"I want this evening to be perfect, a moment that you will remember forever."

"Me too."

"On the way, I have to stop at a few places, check some things, military subjects; you'll have to wait for me."

"I'll be fine."

"Did you bring the diary I gave you?"

"Yes, thank you, it's beautiful. I haven't yet had time to thank you."

"You can draw flowers, as many as you like."

"Yes, thank you, I will." Will you

also take the binoculars with you this time?

Oberst Ernest goes on to talking about the wonderful French wine, telling me about a new crate of bottles he's received especially from Bordeaux, and about the bottle he especially brought for tonight. I smile at him, putting my palm in his hand and thinking of all the women who crowded in line outside the grocery store in the Latin Quarter a few days ago. They were whispering that a shipment of flour had arrived while they waited patiently, hoping it would not end before it was their turn.

"You're quiet today."

"I'm looking at the river view, look at how beautiful it is."

"But today you are especially quiet."

"I thought you liked that about me."

"I liked that, but I would like to know more about you."

"What more would you like to know?"

"I'll be happy to know what's on your mind right now." His palm is still on my thighs as if guarding me, where can I run?

"I'm thinking about the grey clouds ahead of us," I point my head at the grey mass in the sky that awaits us above the horizon. "I hope it doesn't rain."

"Soon we will reach the seashore; you will love the open sea."

✳✳✳

The autumn wind constantly shakes the bushes and weeds on the dirt road, which curves to the seashore. On our way from the nearest village, we pass two army checkpoints which block the beach for the local fishermen, and on either side of the road there are barbed wire fences and concrete bunkers from which machine guns peek out.

"They might come from here," Herr Ernest tells me once as I look out over the trenches, making myself calm and holding the side of the vehicle shaking on the dirt road.

"Why did you stop?" Oberst Ernest asks the driver who slowly slides the vehicle onto the road.

"Look." The driver nods at a brown rabbit standing peacefully among the bushes.

"It's time," Ernest whispers to him, "this time he is mine." Quietly he gets out of the car, and I turn my head to the other side and close my eyes tightly, waiting for the shot to come. But even though I'm ready, my whole body shakes when I hear the sound of gunfire, and I have to stop myself from screaming, leaving my eyes closed.

"Great hunting." I hear his voice and open my eyes, trying to look at the distant sea and ignore Oberst Ernest, who proudly shows the driver the brown, dirty red lump of fur.

"He is big." The driver admires the trophy.

"Yes, we will give it as a gift to the cook at the outpost; he will make lunch out of it." He laughs and sits next to me, slamming the door and signaling for the driver to drive. I can smell the blood.

"Did you see?" He asks me.

"I could not look." What does he expect me to say?

"Hunting is not for women," he puts his gloved hand back on my thighs, and I imagine the lump of fur lying next to the driver and his hand touching it, feeling nauseous.

"Here's the beach and the sea you love so much," he shows me as the driver continues on the winding path towards the scarred sand, striped with barbed wire fences and jagged iron pillars that extend into the stormy sea and the grey waves hitting the shore.

"Heil Hitler." I hear the loud call

from the line of soldiers waiting
for us in a parade, shouting when
the vehicle stops in front of a large
grey concrete bunker.

"Would you like to wait for me in
the car? Or you can go for a walk
around, draw some flowers in your
notebook," he asks me as the local
commander approaches and stands
politely away from the vehicle,
waiting for Oberst Ernest to put on
his officer's hat and say goodbye.

"Can I go around and draw?"

"Yes, but do not approach the edge
of the cliff or try to go down to the
sea." He nods at the beach dotted
with barbed wire fences.

"I will stay away from the sea;
thank you." I tighten the coat
around my body and get away
from the vehicle, turning my back

to the driver who shows the lump of fur to the soldiers. What did the rabbit think as it ate grass? Did it know that its fate was sealed?

***

"What are you doing?"

He is wearing a German soldier uniform, standing above me on the mound, watching with interest as I bend over and hold the camera, trying to quickly shoot a battery of cannons that are well-camouflaged and hidden inside a concrete bunker, dominating the beach.

"I'm taking a picture."

"Photography is not allowed here, who are you?"

I am a young woman who is soon going to end her life with severe torture because she was stupid, arrogant, and careless. My legs are shaking, and I want to scream, or start running and throw myself on the barbed wire fences surrounding the cliff overlooking the sea.

"I'm a photographer for SIGNAL, your army magazine, do you know it? So I'm allowed," I answer him in perfect German as I get up, trying to smile my most peaceful smile at him, praying he doesn't notice my trembling legs.

"Really? So why were you bending over?"

"How much can you photograph army stuff? Sometimes I also want to photograph flowers, come and see." And he lowers the barrel

471

of the rifle which was pointed in my direction, hanging it over his shoulder, and approaches me suspiciously. I can smell his strong body odor mixed with the stench of cigarettes and sweat.

"It's beautiful. You have talent." He admires the drawings in my diary, speaking in poor German.

"Thanks."

"Where are you from?"

"Now Paris, before that Berlin, where are you from?" Please let him be from another city.

"Now Normandy, before that Gdańsk."

"You were not born in Germany?"

"No, I'm Polish, I was recruited by force, they needed soldiers, and

Slava needed food and cigarettes.
It's always better to be on the
winning side."

"Always better."

"Want one?" He offers me a simple
cigarette, smiling toothlessly.

"No thanks." I smile at him; I have
to get out of here.

"Wait here, don't move." He turns
his back to me, disappearing
beyond the mound, and my legs
are trembling again; what to do?
Where can I escape?

"Here, now take a picture."
Slava returns, standing in front
of me, trying to tuck his shirt
into his pants and arrange his
uniform while holding a bunch of
wildflowers he just picked.

"Watch out for the barbed wire fences on the cliff; there are mines there." He salutes me goodbye with his toothless smile, leaving me alone among the hills, holding a bunch of wildflowers in my hand and sweating under my dress, despite the autumn wind.

***

"Monique, where are you? " I hear Ernest's call among the sandy mounds, and I freeze in place; this time, I pushed too hard. The camera is in my hand, and my little bag has been left behind, along with the open diary.

"Monique." I can hear him getting closer.

"Don't come here."

"Monique."

"Don't come here." How do I release the film? What did he explain to me in the basement? Which button to press?

"What are you doing?"

"What every woman should sometimes do in private." Is that the button? Now turn the knob? I'm not sure anymore, is that what he explained to me? I have to hurry.

"Are you alright?"

"Yes, I'm fine, please don't come here." Here, that knob, now take the film out of the camera, where's the release button? Please don't slip out of my hands; it's stuck, by force, release it already.

"I'm waiting for you here."

"Thanks, I'm already done." What to do with the film? Where to hide it? And what about the camera?

"Are you okay? You should not have gone so far; there are minefields around here, I started worrying about you." Herr Ernest approaches me as he holds my bag in his hand, looking politely to the side, as I step out from behind a bush and arrange my dress.

"I looked at your diary; I hope you don't mind." He hands me my bag and the open diary. "I enjoy them."

"Do you like them?"

"Are you okay? Your hands are dirty from the ground."

"Yeah, I'm fine, I stumbled when I

climbed the hill, it's nothing." I rub my hands together and take the bag and the diary from his hands while smiling at him, hoping he won't notice that I'm sweating. The film's metal box is scratching my thighs, buried inside my panties.

"Have you finished your military things here? Are we going to the car?"

"You shouldn't have gone so far, it's dangerous, I'm done here, now we'll go to the hotel, it's already getting late."

On the dirt road back from
the beach to the quiet village,
Oberst Ernest and the driver
are reminded of the rabbit. With
shouts of 'Schnell, Schnell' the
driver accelerates on the white
road, chasing an imaginary rabbit.

While Oberst Ernest smiles at me, I'm smiling back, thinking of the German camera which remains under a bush on the shores of Normandy, covered in a bit of dirt which I was able to stack with my palms.

"Are you excited about tonight?" he asks me. "I booked us a table for dinner."

***

My fingers gently hold the pink napkin as I wipe my lips and place it in the corner of the table.

"Did the meal taste good to you?"

"The meal was delicious, thank you."

"Shall we go upstairs?"

478

"Can we take a walk on the promenade by the sea?"

"It's dark outside and cold, don't you want us to go up? The room is waiting for us."

"I'll be happy to take a walk."

While we are leaving the dining room of the luxurious hotel, I turn around and look back. All the tables are full of high-ranking German officers, accompanied by women like me; maybe Herr Ernest will see a fellow officer here who will be glad to start a conversation?

"Shall we go?"

The clerk at reception hurries to bring my coat at the sight of Oberst Ernest's hand, and I give a last look at the warm dining room, heading outside.

The cold wind on the promenade surprises me as we walk side by side silently, and I'm trying to hug myself, keep distant from him.

"Are you cold?"

"No, I like the winter wind."

We are the only ones along the dark beach, whether because of the winter or the war. Here, too, barbed wire fences stretch along the Black Coast, and only the sound of the waves can be heard in the distance.

"Heil Hitler," a guard emerges alert from a guard station, but when he notices Ernest's ranks, he stands still and salutes, ignoring me.

"Heil Hitler," Ernest answers him and releases him to his concrete shelter, leaving us alone again on the deserted windy boardwalk.

"Shall we go back to the hotel?" Herr Ernest asks after a few minutes. "The bottle of wine I brought is waiting for us in the room."

"Yes, let's go back to the hotel." My time has come.

***

The silk pantyhose repeatedly slips from my thighs as I try to close the garter buckle on it, getting tangled with my trembling fingers.

"Shall I pour you the wine?" I can hear Oberst Ernest from the bedroom.

"Yes, please."

I also don't like the white lace underwear, and I blush when I try to arrange it so that I am more comfortable, avoiding looking at myself in the mirror in the dim light of the bathroom lamp.

"Can you please light candles?"

"But this hotel has electricity."

"Please."

"The wine is waiting for us."

"I'll be out in a minute."

I hope he doesn't notice my hesitant steps, or my unsteady hand holding the wine glass, trying to sip it in one gulp and feeling a drop land on my white lingerie, probably leaving a red stain on it.

"You are so beautiful; I was waiting for you. Come closer to me; it will not hurt."

Philip, I'll think of Philip. I have memorized that dozens of times in the last days, but no matter how hard I try, Philip has disappeared from my thoughts into the darkness of the basement of the Latin Quarter. All I can think of now is a woman lying on her back in a fancy hotel room on the big bed, moaning from pain and his body weight.

That's it; I'm a French prostitute who has slept with a German officer.

***

End of Part 1

Printed in Great Britain
by Amazon

18707568R00281